~STORIES OF CLASSY EROTICA~

LASCIVIOUS
ROMANTICISM
"THE BOOK OF SHANGRI-LA"

CARLOS "THE POET B.GKL" KAIGLER

~Stories Of Classy Erotica~
Lascivious Romanticism
"The Book Of Shangri-La"
Copyright © 2025 Carlos V. Kaigler

Printed in the United States of America

ISBN-13: 979-8-9897973-0-1

Cover & Interior Design:
Carlos V. Kaigler /C'vaughn'K Graphic Designs/ Author The Poet B.GKL

Website:
www.authorbgkl.com
www.cvaughnk.com

Sites:
https://linktr.ee/Thepoet_BrothaGKL
https://linktr.ee/MrAndMrsKaigler
https://linktr.ee/CvaughnKphotography

Email:
Thepoet-b.gkl@hotmail.com

Business:
C'vaughn'K Graphic Designs
(313) 334-9630

Author The Poet B.GKL Definition:

Yoni- *The essence of women's universal life-giver and love.*
Gawddess- *Infinite goddess form of a Kween aka Queen in power.*
Kween- *The truest form of the real Queen.*
Keenng- *The truest form of the real King.*
Gaia-tize- *Mothered and one with the earth.*

The Poet
B. GKL

Brotha GKL / Gawd Keenny L io' EF

ACKNOWLEDGMENTS

My Beautiful Ultimate Kween Wife, ***Charnissa V. Kaigler*** you are the universe that surrounds me with your fluorescent love, and I thank you for the encouragement you give me with every craft I choose to master and then some. My wife, you are like the lit candle to my darkness and the cure to my realm of desolate past days and I love you to life and respect the romance we share that is deeper than the physical flesh. You are my bliss and I thank you for helping me brainstorm through my legion of scattered ideas puzzling in its creative chaos and also helping me get out of my mind to see clearly, I am thankful to have you as my wife, best friend, and soul bond.

I made it my life goal to publish powerful books in some of my favorite book genres like Action & Adventure, Mystery, Horror, Thriller & Suspense, and Romance just to name a few. Erotica on the other hand has always been a genre that called to me the way that poetry and spoken word have done in so many ways, and it's a mystery to me how the genre of erotica calls to me so in-depth. My erotic writing path was influenced even deeper down the road by another legendary author that so many great people that were in my life talked highly of, the prestigious legend and bestselling Author ***Zane***, her books are masterpieces to me in every way. In my own opinion, ***Zane*** has mastered her unique style of erotica and took the erotic writing style to another level and I respect her for all that she does and achieve. My mission is to bring my erotic flavor to all romantic sensualist eyes of the reading world as she has with her wonderful works of written art; ***Zane*** will always be considered erotic royalty of the craft with so many other skills I honor.

I have written so many erotic pieces to the point I decided to dedicate this book to Nature and every mature person who is Married, Engaged, Dating, a Bachelorette or Bachelor, Polygamist, Alone, Heartbroken, the healing & healed, and those in life that inner stand true intimacy beyond the body and mind and many other beautiful walks of love. Being intimate is much more profound and can be expressed in all ways and should be over stood with an open mind with respect. I think all of my powerful positive Ancestors & Guides that mean me well in my path of the unseen and seen; I thank them for never judging my purpose but allowing me to be me. I appreciate and thank all the people who as genuinely shown me love and built bonds with me through my growth and inner standing of who I became today… I love you all to life.

Sincerely, **Carlos "The Poet B.GKL" Kaigler aka Brotha GKL/ Gawd Keenng Lio'lf**

~STORIES OF CLASSY EROTICA~

LASCIVIOUS ROMANTICISM
"THE BOOK OF SHANGRI-LA"

The Poet

B. GKL

Brotha GKL / Gawd Keenng L io'Cf

CONTENTS

DEDICATION

The direction of fine roots that grew this book was manifested from the vibe of one of my short narrated classy erotic poems... titled:

Lascivious Romanticism

Compelled by the silver drips of a heart leaking over my brass veins.

Rain dripping on our blaze embracing the sweetness for hazel brown slithers of clashing skin.

Her bend, her curve, her urge to transcend the compulsive need to chain my soul to her scrumptious spread.

Lead by the immortal energy of my craving to taste a moment of immense *Shangri-La*.

~B.GKL

"Poetic Spoken Tales"
The Infinite Mind Of Lio'lf
Publication date: May 4, 2021

DEFINITIONS

Lascivious: *[luh-siv-ee-uhs]*
driven by lust; preoccupied with or exhibiting lustful desires.

Romanticism: an exciting and mysterious quality.

Shangri-La: any place or complete bliss and delight and peace.

STORY 1:
Ms. Dulcet's Jewelry Store

STORY 1
Ms. Dulcet's Jewelry Store

Definition:

Dulcet- *extremely pleasant in a gentle way, very pleasing to the ear.*

Yoni- *The essence of women's universal life-giver and love.*

Gawddess- *Infinite goddess form of a Kween aka Queen in power.*

Characters:
Ms. Dulcet, Mr. Rival and **Sensualist Oshun**

The Monday glare of the sun opened my eyes with its shifting heat as it cased between the apartment blinds, my brown skin enjoyed the blazing supper of spreading light clothing my entire resting body landscaped across the leather lounge.

Watching the rays scrounging around my place examining it for gloomy corners standing without its brilliance. I feel the beautiful resilience as my back sets up against the sofa, feeling the boredom settle in with only one warmth on my mind... **Ms. Dulcet** from the jewelry store yesterday. The way she persists with her criminal-like aroma holding my sense of smell captive, scent loafing around in my shirt and linen scarf. I yawned heavily and started walking to my bedroom towards my shower to wash away the memories of her from my physique. My body feels a mourning of not having more of her liveness with me now within this vapor.

Every cosmic acre of **Ms. Dulcet's** visual being has left a trace of her saccharine utterance screeching through my drenched skin tone of copper. Thoughts of her soft-spoken cheekbones sliding across my mind while turning off my shower spray, and slowly dressing my soul with addictive oils and an outfit that could start a new day.

Halfway out of the door I noticed I was now rushing, and almost forgot to grab a pleasing excuse to see **Ms. Dulcet**; so, I decided to go get some of my jewelry, placing them in a cream bag to get a deep cleanse for my precious stones. I then walked down the stairwell out the exit towards the curb of the street. Only to then flag down the most luscious female taxi driver in town, a very familiar lewd woman who went by the name **Sensualist Oshun**.

A bosomy beauty with the intensity of a true royal soul. The cabs atmosphere was always balanced with essential herbs, and soft body creams to arouse the instincts of a classy gentleman like myself. I couldn't help but be mesmerized every time I caught **Sensualist Oshun's** taxi towards whatever location I was heading that day, plus she always greets me with class along with flirtatious attire and body language that was full of overriding spice. She then greeted me twice as her courtesy sounds muffled upon closing the door as I gazed, and she beautifully replied: ***"Grand risings to you love one, and where would you like to travel upon today, sweetheart."*** I then tried to speak after I snapped out of her spell-bound radiance of pristine enchantment. The smooth bass of my raspy accent spoke the words... **"Grand rising Sensualist Oshun, please take me to Ms. Dulcet's jewelry store my dearie.** With a voice like a canary, she begins to sing the words... *"Let's get a move on it then Mr. Rival."*

As I watched the tidal of rivers in her divination of eyes from the mirror as she drove, the road turned into a traffic jam with only twenty minutes in between us and the jewelry store. Before I was able to check the meter, **Sensualist Oshun** placed her right hand over the meter with a smile, and she voiced to me gently... *"Mr. Rival, there's no need for you to trouble yourself with a fee today because time is yours, my mocha love."* I began to ask why but then she whispered a sweet command... *"Suppress your lips at once in my cab, and unwind for the moment... because we may be in this traffic jam for a while."* She then whispered even slower but more honeyed... *"Mr. Rival I know that you have a tendency to want me without knowing that you love toothsome bodies molded into a curvy deluxe."*

When I looked at **Sensualist Oshun** after hearing her words as my aura reeked of in denial and confusion, as I watched this hard-working woman telling me to decompress and elevate my patience. So, I lowered my impatience towards getting to **Ms. Dulcet's...** yet enchanted once more by the destiny of **Sensualist Oshun's** amorous ways of making obstacles feel erotically casual. The actual tinted windows on her cab started to become darker than licorice, and the neo-soul ambient music then slowed down with an intimately sorcerous flavor.

Watching her devour all worries of all things, she ignores her surroundings while she caters to my sight. Traffic was moving yet again nowhere else but jammed as I continued to try to ignore her beguiling mantrap preserves. **Sensualist Oshun** lays back in her driver's seat and slides down her intimate coral of colored apparel from beneath her yellow skirt as her eyelids descend into two slow winks. The Plexiglas steamed from the backseat as she decorated the dashboard with her soothing under garments with the cab meter reading four-hundred and forty-four dollars. As the traffic stood still and stayed inactive around her gold and black taxi full of rare fragrances lingering about; I felt that she was trying to keep me hooked.

She looked at me from the rearview mirror with enough aspect to remove a perfect crease from my right pants leg. I was shifting in my seat as the music became mellowed to my ears, and she then glides her skirt high passed her hip line; I watched her body go into slow movements of smooth rhythms to the stereo's soulful melodies. I leaned forward and spoke deeply through the cash slot with a question.

"Is this dance a nutriment for my conquest or for many travelers that come into your machine of enticement?"

Sensualist Oshun turned slightly to me with the purest smile which was like white icing, and lips soft as chocolate dahlia flowers; she placed both of her knees in the driver's seat as she faced me in her yellow risen skirt and missing inner silk. I watched her leather heels hit the mat on the floor as she placed her left knee in the passenger seat over the arm rest, then she unlocked the medium-sized Plexiglas window between us. *Sensualist Oshun* spoke to me in the manner of a woman full of polite demands, and in need of her daily tease of spontaneous evoking as she speaks softly through the open Plexiglas.

"Mr. Rival, I respect you as a true gentleman but today I wish for you to be what I need for this brief occasion. I shall never be touched by your hands but I will allow the pressure of your voice to hold a part of my breathing; to savor the taste from the earth of my two cushioned servings freed from the support fabric of my back hooks… just waiting for me to release permission to them upon your tender nibble."

As I looked at *Sensualist Oshun,* just moving like smoke from a blown candle. My hands were indocile, and reaching for both sides of the Plexiglas from the back seat as my fingers spread open like a deck of cards just waiting for her to see my next move. Right before the movements of foreplay were jazzing my bones as I nudged forward face first to the window waiting for her encounter.

I then heard the sound of her unmentionables snap from her middle back before *Sensualist Oshun's* fingers could twist and descend the fabric hold to her under sides. Watching her rip her shirt from the middle split down from under her gold key on her necklace as my face stood still from the back looking through the square of the Plexiglas window. She looked me in the soul of my eyes as she withdrew from the rip shirt of her shoulders, and tossed the restraints that hardly was holding what my lips now were waiting for.

She through more clothing to the car dashboard for more decoration, and used her left hand to reach for my neck to pull herself closer into the middle of her void of hating distance. Her right hand disappeared above the arm rest complimenting her as she channeled the *Yoni's* vision of what lies beyond the yellow skirt. *Sensualist Oshun* becomes dedicated to reaching the cosmos, as I drowned passionately upon her soft planets wanting to land but respecting her fetish of being untouched by what she desires for one to grasp. She looks up at me grabbing the back of my mind with her left hand pressing my thoughts deeper into her cleavage; she elevates past the moment speaking another set of words to me as she looks down into my meaning as she speaks the next step.

"Mr. Rival, I am now giving you the option of comfort for me to unlatch this full Plexiglas from my side or I could just continue to bait you until the road has motion once more. Kiss one part of my flesh once if you would love for me to unlatch the full glass or kiss one part of my skin twice to continue this enticement of a tease."

Then I looked at her in her face like a hunter waiting to feed its hunger. I am one who does not play with my dinner nor my time so I kissed her flesh once, and I set back in my seat to watch her hands become free as she removed both latches to the full Plexiglas. She was ready to make things more difficult for my ride to *Ms. Dulcet's Jewelry Store* to get my merchandise cleaned.

Sensualist Oshun looked at me grinning while moistening her top lip. She then climbs over the opening of the Plexiglas window to the backseat on to my torso: both of her knees were piercing the leather seats on the side of my thighs. I grabbed both of her wrists while placing *Sensualist Oshun's* rhythmic pulse behind her life structure. Pinning her wrist crossed against her lower back sacrum with my left hand as she rolled her saucy eyes; I pulled my cream linen shirt completely from myself with my right hand as she leaned in to taste a morsel of my pectus. I pushed her soft-held hands into her back to make things known that my dominance has control as of this moment upon her permission to give her completeness to me.

Giving her my vision of what shall now be done at this moment of thirst that acquires no cup. I am neither dehydrated nor anxious yet just ready to let things pour from one button unleashed. As my right hand begins releasing my cargo shorts; my boxer briefs and shorts then become acquainted with my ankles. While one of my feet slid from my sandal allowing me to maneuver one leg over to give more movement to this random destiny. *Sensualist Oshun* feels my over standing rising as she gets familiar with the darkness of my phallus while placing the lambskin shield upon it to protect our forthcoming. *Sensualist Oshun* has been guiding me into the idea of what the *Yoni* was in need of within so many luxe hints of bluntness. Now she slides her existence over the key to provoke the full nature bestowed near the door itself. I then released her hands and placed them around the back of my hair line as I rotated the key to perform the open motion from the sealed domain. As the doors open, and her house streams unquestionable sweetish waters; her earth begins to shift her foundation to the structure of my certainty.

Her bosoms filled my mouth like the air that holds itself in the jaws before the lungs could ever take the wind. Her yellow skirt ascends and falls to her toes like a Persian Buttercup plucked in the storm of my lightning towards the belly of this ride. My hands imprint the grip of my fingers on to her melon round bottom of voluptuous sweets. The back seat became the rawness of both our attentions as our skin began sweating out our libido without any mention of the traffic that had not moved an inch. It was almost as if time itself owed *Sensualist Oshun* a favor and everything felt motionless around us.

Our breath painted a portrait of carnal steam on the windows from the lungs of me. Her body drag raced our pulse into the destination of one of the most poetic collisions. The golden key on her necklace begins to rise and fall against the brown sugared gap between the buxom breathing lines of her chest. The pleasant region of her posterior nitty-gritty just bull riding my pelvis into the taxi's seating without any disconnection between my touch and her own.

Sensualist Oshun removes her warmhearted hands from my hair line as she places her arms across one another compressing a clutch of her own body. Grasping herself tightly as the sound of trapped cars full of anger and muffled blowing horns of impatience grew trumpet-like. The way she released the hold on herself to eloquently run her warm hands alongside both of my deltoids; she then felt the tension under my skin as my handled grip held on to her posterior. Her motion jackhammers above the caress, as I set underneath her destruction placed upon me.

I began to settle *Sensualist Oshun's* brown sugar soul with my propulsion to ground her stir of electricity electrifying our current situation. As we sat surrounded by bodies of cars with enraged drivers fueling in heat over a traffic jam. The taxi that we are in felt unseen in the condition of being in the blurred naked eye without a witness to judge me or *Sensualist Oshun.* While within a place of enticing one another behind foggy windows with only minutes between us and *Ms. Dulcets Jewelry Store. Sensualist Oshun* then begins to tremble through the fullness of reaching the intimate goal as my energy becomes captive within the lambskin shield. She then looked me in my eyes while placing her finger tips upon my oblique's as I and her both gave up one mild breath from our lungs in completion; we then noticed one lane of cars beginning to move, and far ahead all traffic was starting to become free.

Sensualist Oshun smiled while quickly reaching for a sundress from her bag in the passenger seat. She then climbed back to the front in a rush of enjoyment as the cars blew loudly behind us to move along, and we drove off slowly as she spoke to me from the front as I got dressed and closed the Plexiglas behind her.

"Mr. Rival, how about we head to my loft not too far from Ms. Dulcets Jewelry Store so that we both can get cleaned up and refreshed? I give you my word that I will not distract you any longer afterward, let me get you to your destination; also before you answer that, I must answer the question you asked me earlier that I replied to with only a smile. You asked if this dance was a nutriment for your conquest or for many travelers that come along my machine of enticement; well, no. I am just a classy woman who's picky and knows what I want when I want it. I paid close attention to the way

you carried yourself upon many other times I picked you up, and every time you entered my cab, I held my intimate desires towards you to myself. I'm not explaining all this to you to reach a serious relationship but to express that a Gawddess deserves whatever fruit she wants where ever she feels her kingdom is under her feet. So, what do you say?"

As **Sensualist Oshun** continued to drive, the way she looked back at me was well-favored, and her question had been asked and waiting for my answer. While I got dressed in the back seat contemplating my determination of something that is already in the works; I spoke to **Sensualist Oshun** as I checked my watch for the time, and I smiled as I reclined my body back with a coquetry tone of yes touching her ear drums. **Sensualist Oshun** then accelerated miles ahead with her music still felt upon me like Caribbean Sea waters splashing away the impurities with her serene touch. Thinking to myself about **Sensualist Oshun**, one would misunderstand her approach for lust but she is the essence of observance and a hunter for one kind of prey that has class without any fear within it. In her eyes I can see that the world could never murder her choices to live as nature intended; free from scrutiny, and all the lonely captive hearts chained to broken traditions and judgmental tongues.

So, at this point, my curiosity was itching to reach her residence but right after my thought we arrived at a glass building of lofts; it felt as if she placed her ears to my thoughts to hear me speak about her mysterious actions at hand. Before I could open my mouth, a suited gentleman approached her door to open it while helping her out of the car; he retrieved her keys to then sat behind the wheel while waiting for me to walk from it, **Sensualist Oshun** then waved for me to get out of the car to follow her. As I got out, I grabbed my cream bag, and I walked over to stand next to her as **Sensualist Oshun's** craving aroma pulled me in slowly with the surroundings of all of her light around us; a ravishing building stood in front of us reflecting the cities sun from its glass and brick foundation of lofts to the sky.

She began walking ahead of me but time didn't just move slowly like the movies but more like a projector flickering in a black and white choppy set of lights, with movements of her sundress dancing left and right; the way she stepped was like a leopard walking a thin tree branch to slumber at its highest point and showing off every single mold of her natural soul. As we both make it to the building door passing the empty lobby and towards the upstairs to the second floor... *Sensualist Oshun* began to speak as we walked down her hallway."

"Mr. Rival, you seem like a man that lives inside of his head but today I want you to invite me into your very being as we allow each other to clean each other's bodies with time; I'm sure your jewelry won't get any dirtier than they already are. So, here is my place, loft "118."

Sensualist Oshun started unlocking her door and then I felt the feelings of elation from other doors in the hall as if this building was full of flawlessness. Before I could step into *Oshun's* loft a woman a way down walked out of her loft with the symbol of *Ms. Dulcets Jewelry Store* embossed on her blazer sleeve. Before I could get a clear look at her face, *Sensualist Oshun* pulled me in by the shoulders closing the door behind us, and then she took my cream bag from my hand while telling me the shower was running. I looked at her while figuring to myself *Oshun* was not one to be ignored as her sundress painted the floor as it fell like a canvas of living art across the room's woodgrain of echoes. The volume of her standing here in the center of her royalty with her afro plum choked by the cross of her legs twisted in a pose.

I froze in captivation as I walked in glitches of staggering steps toward *Sensualist Oshun* while dropping my attire to the floor in a trance. *Sensualist Oshun* guided me behind her saunter towards the rain shower to manifest the other side of her true ritzy romance. We clenched our bodies in a slow brew of Tantric foreplay, learning to over stand the intimacy of our hands, our minds, and our souls grasping our needs with just the subtle touches. Water fell to our crowns and down to our faces past the root energy of our beginnings. *Sensualist Oshun* and I then immediately inner stood the facts of just letting go; we genuinely held one another on a superior tier beyond the plane of two rich mocha dreams mixing a tasteful reality.

{As Sensualist Oshun and Mr. Rival stood in the water ripples of one another, a Goldfinch decided to rest its feathers on the bathroom outside window ledge; as this melodic bird began to sing from its

well-tuned body of nature taking in every air of notes written through the glass into the rain shower.

Along with the natural mountain feel of Mr. Rival's entire being leaning into Sensualist Oshun; her magnificent earth fills this loft with a pleasant land fill of powerful chocolate tones of dainty sweetness. Sensualist Oshun then turns to grab a bottle of her edible handmade body wash to create a soft ganja froth within her hands as she squeezes out a large amount to hand wash his layers. Hemp suds fell from her fingers as she coated Mr. Rival's full position patiently; she took more of the body wash to lather her skin like candle wax creeping down a copper holder under heat. Mr. Rival stands at peace in the middle of pure elation as Sensualist Oshun speaks to his eyes instead of his ears with five words.}

"Mr. Rival, Kneel to me."

{Mr. Rival glanced down into her royal eyes with his decision already made for what's next, and then the sound of a mountain repositioning its great shift as his one left knee embraced the shower floor as the right knee stood forward like a single step. Sensualist Oshun then takes her left foot to stand on his knee as she steps to his breathing throat as her right and left leg wrap around his neck like a plush scarf in the rain. She then bends her back into a Scorpion yoga pose with her ankles crossed loosely around Mr. Rival's neck with the heel of her feet barely touching his spine.

The twine of Sensualist Oshun spoke volumes as Mr. Rival held her pose with his full body strength; as the rain shower became a deep ocean mist as drips of water trickled down his sideburns and she became a nourishment for his soul. Sensualist Oshun's Scorpion yoga pose allowed her to look under and past her shoulder blades to gaze back at his kneeling body of rips. She focused on his masculine pride as he kneeled upon the face of her cliff edge to be pulled in and appreciated. Mr. Rival spoke wisely to her Yoni with grace as she cooled off his blood flow as both souls trembled with the touch of romantic lashing and loving.

Mr. Rival then lifted his mind from the wisdom of her thighs, and Sensualist Oshun then came out of her Scorpion yoga pose as she

23

set on his shoulders with her eyes closed; as edible hemp body wash covered their flesh as the soaring high had now entered their wet pores. Mr. Rival removes the doors of her legs to return them both to standing face to face after a showcase of bending bodies behind a shower glass. Mr. Rival then pulled her close to him to let his words flow into her relaxed face as the shower waters roared down on them.}

Sensualist Oshun, I do not over stand the poetic pull that you have over my curiosity or my cane that waits at the pelvis of my fondness; you are just an exuberant *Kween* that is too difficult for me to deny! However, I cannot allow one so picturesque and libidinous to drain the rest of what fuel I have left in the flesh of my stance. It seems that I was just drawn to you from my home, to your taxi, and into the realms of your ever-lush soul.

{Sensualist Oshun then smiles and looks at Mr. Rival with the thought of someone enjoying the bitten burst of fresh pineapple juices falling from the corners of one's mouth. The entire time Mr. Rival spoke, the shower glazed over them as they stood together soaking in positive karma. As he laced her attention with the low-pitched penetration of his voice to her mind, she held his every word passed the humid waters that lingered in lazy drips from his lips as he spoke to Sensualist Oshun. His right hand rubbed around to her pelvic arch as the left hand massaged the crown of her soft wooly hair dripping from the scalp with the eyes of Medusa holding him in the stone of motionless elegance. Mr. Rival then speaks from the depth to keep his self-focus.}

"Sensualist Oshun, damn it beloved one, you are an ambrosial masterpiece but I must be on my way, this was a gratifying altered addition to the plans I made for today."

{Oshun's enchanting smile burrowed the gaze of joy throughout the ambiance of the bathroom as she reached over to turn off the shower. The last remaining suds dissolve from the flesh as the showerhead empties its last drips from the copper pipes as they stand in the draining water collecting their thoughts. The singing Goldfinch was done resting its feathers outside the window and decided to take flight towards its next ballad of bird songs for

another set of romantics. Mr. Rival placed honorable kisses upon both her shoulders as he stepped out the shower glass door to grab two drying towels from its stack. She then steps out moments after as he decides to throw his towel over his head and begins to pat dry the wetness from her body as she stands facing him. Honoring every part of her domain, he drips to the floors with chivalry racing through the strength of his hands as Sensualist Oshun feels the energy force of his palms from the other side of the plush drying towel.

Sensualist Oshun looks at Mr. Rival patting her body dry; she gazes at him like a soul of fresh air. She does not see him as a piece of meat but more of a powerful gardener maintaining the landscape of her earth from top to bottom without any concern for the sweltering heat. After Mr. Rival finished drying her body, he leaned over to kiss the left corner of her full lips as he turned away with the grin of a tease while leaving her towel in her hands.

Mr. Rival walked down the hall drying himself off and walking towards the living room as the words bare skin warrior was written in her eyes as she watched him walk away. She stood unclothed holding her damp towel releasing a short laugh and smacking her lips while reaching for her gold sheer kaftan. Sensualist Oshun walks from the bathroom into the living room with the sun sending a trail of light through the window revealing what was already seen through the sheers of her kaftan. Mr. Rival stood fully clothed with is thoughts pleasurably captivated all over again, watching Oshun walk towards the freezer for ice cubes to crunch; the sun glared through her sheer kaftan making her beautiful stretch marks glow from her back thighs up to her soft fundament. Mr. Rival then spoke his mind.}

Sensualist Oshun, I have to force myself to leave your presence if I am ever to make it to my destination before Ms. Dulcet's jewelry store closes at some point beloved. I will catch the subway the rest of the way, no need to drop me off, I am sure you have seen enough of me for today.

{Sensualist Oshun crunched down on her last piece of ice as she listened to Mr. Rival speak with her poker face and decided to cut

his words off like a Chef's knife cutting through a dripping steak.}

"Mr. Rival, we must have an over standing between us, I am a bachelorette with an unusual class but I am adventurous and very omnipotent. I can tell that you are a bachelor with complex taste and I can see your magnificent gentleman's aura; I am not an obstacle but a clear solution of positive opportunities. With that being said, take the damn keys off my countertop and handle your business darling… whatever that may be but just bring back my property in the same condition given to you. Before you ask me, why in the hell would I trust in you this way is because I am gifted enough to read your energy and I always trust my instincts. So, get your jewels polished at Ms. Dulcets Jewelry Store, and don't waste any more time defying my voice of logic."

{Mr. Rival just stood there in a bit of confusion as he glanced over at the keys laying on the counter top; he looked over at Sensualist Oshun. She then walks to her vinyl album collection to play some Neo-Soul on her record player; Oshun grabs a small marble egg next to her albums on the shelf near her favorite chair by the window. Mr. Rival stood in contemplation about the keys as he watched Sensualist Oshun pull out a perfectly pre-rolled joint from the marble egg and place a flame to its end; clouds of smoke caressed her lips as she blew out some Mary jane slowly to then look over at Mr. Rival to say something. Yet he was speechless as she spoke once more to motivate an odd moment toward clarity.}

"Mr. Rival, relax, I am a different type of Kween and I meant what I said before… go have fun, and do not forget to grab your cream bag of jewels in my vase by the front door. Just remember to bring my wheels back to its Kween later today and knock when you make it back so I can let you in."

{Mr. Rival then smirked with an obscure gaze and turned to grab the keys and towards the door while grabbing his cream bag from the vase and out into the hall way. As the door closed behind Mr. Rival a saccharine whiff of hemp gifted its aroma from the doors closing clenched into its locked position as he paused while taking in a deep breath of clearness.

As he walked from Sensualist Oshun's door and down the hall as her neo-soul became fainter to his ears but felt by the soul of his ruling steps of something he as conquered but valued. From the hall and down to the second floor and out the building to her taxi he looks up at her window to see Sensualist Oshun's toes basking outside her window under the sun as her toe rings glare from the ray's touch. Smoke flowing from her window as it sends out smokey signals of divine peace as Mr. Rival turns away to get in the car to drive towards Ms. Dulcets Jewelry Store. He then threw his cream bag of jewels in the passenger seat as the tires cruised on.

As he drove, the smell of Sensualist Oshun's soft oiled perfume lingered with her scent trapped in the headrest, the steering wheel, and all that she may have touched; it all sent a gratifying quiver down his spine. As he drove, the pure thought of Sensualist Oshun became more riddled through his mind with thought streams of her forming a ravine in his soul. Mr. Rival then clears his throat with a grunt and gets his bachelor mindset back into focus but for some reason, he couldn't over stand why he encountered so many major delays in his plans for today. Ms. Dulcet then popped into his mind heavily as he finally arrived at the front curb of Ms. Dulcet's Jewelry Store. Mr. Rival drowns out the battle of noise around him as the sidewalk and street overflowed like rivers of fresh fish jumping and traveling in the same motion... rushing to no end.

Mr. Rival cuts the engine and grabs his cream bag from the passenger seat and steps out of the taxi. He looked in the store windows hoping to spot Ms. Dulcet at the front counter but she was nowhere to be seen. Mr. Rival then strolls around the car on to the sidewalk to enter the door with gentle bells sounding his entry. He then assumes Ms. Dulcet must be in the back somewhere as he decides to look around at other jewelry with a feeling of uncertainty. Mr. Rival clings to his deep thoughts about even coming to Ms. Dulcets Jewelry Store after the impact of Sensualist Oshun's presence and taking him far beyond his romance by purely arousing his nature. Ms. Dulcet then walks from the back curtains holding her briefcase to leave for lunch as she spots Mr. Rival looking down at her store's finest timepieces. Ms. Dulcet walked out to the floor to get Mr. Rival's attention as she walked near him as her fragrance of strawberries with a hint of elegant champagne rumba danced through his nose as she spoke to his assumed ego.}

Hello Mr. Rival, does the point of time interest you more than the arms of something that could appreciate every moment of you being here today? I knew that you would come back to me at some point. I don't mean to sound so sure of myself but when you are a woman of high morality and standards you learn the ways of what anyone wants or needs... especially for a woman in my career choice who has to pay attention to remarkable details of all jewels presented.

{Mr. Rival finally looked over at Ms. Dulcet but not with the look that she may have wanted but the expression of a man full of agitation, miscalculated thoughts, and adjustment; he then spoke to her with completion.}

"Well, Ms. Dulcet, I guess you have all your knowledge prepared for a man like myself but I am not to be mastered but inner stood; I know that every moment of me waking up today was full of directions and distractions that require more of my hold. Ms. Dulcet, I don't mean to sound rude towards your overconfidence but I know now that I must leave here with all that I came with. So, enjoy your lunch beloved one, and be at peace."

{Ms. Dulcet looked at him so hard that Mr. Rival could damn near feel her claws shredding through his being with anger by refusing her flirtatious fury; then the store phone rang and Ms. Dulcets employee notified her that her husband Mr. Dulcet has arrived and waiting outside to take her to lunch. Mr. Rival looked a bit shocked about what her employee just said as he then spoke to Ms. Dulcet with a surprised grin.}

"Well damn, Mrs.... Dulcet, you never told me that you were married along with me never seeing a ring on your finger but I guess that shit doesn't even matter at this point my dear lulu of venomous sweetness. Ha-ha... well, don't forget to put your loose ring back on your lying ass finger before you go out to your naive husband. I would have never dealt with your ass period if I know you were married. That shit goes against every moral of my existence as a real man but I now see why my day as been truly odd in the past hours that I have awakened with plans to see you

28

and get my jewelry cleaned. I thought you were a single woman that was ready to play around a bit but just enjoy your got damn lunch and be at ease with your toxic beauty."

{Mrs. Dulcet stood aroused but unbothered in silence while standing her ground with her eyebrow burning through the ceiling with irritation. Mr. Rival turned his back and walked out the front door with the cement ground holding his feet study as he walked to the car with his bag in his hand. Mr. Rival saw nothing in his thoughts but the powerful pull of Sensualist Oshun and all that she had seen in him from just a few rides toward his destinations. Their moment was deeper than just a passionate escapade but more of what Sensualist Oshun put on his higher self. Sensualist Oshun used her chaotic romance on Mr. Rival in which her methods could never be confused with coquette ways but a Kween's desire to conquer what she wants in life without any ridicule or judgment.

Mr. Rival set in the car contemplating, just sitting in the moment in front of Ms. Dulcet's Jewelry Store. Mrs. Dulcet stood inside her store hesitant to come out while waiting for Mr. Rival to drive away without causing her any problems with her husband. Mr. Rival made the decision to not interfere with things that would reveal themselves in time, and he started the car and drove off while shaking his head toward her as he drove. Sensualist Oshun then ran through his thoughts nonstop as he drove back to her now knowing that he was naive for driving to Ms. Dulcets Jewelry Store. As the air blew through the open car windows pushing Sensualist Oshun's sweet scent further into his nose, enough to make a man receive a speeding ticket as a gift towards his urgency to get back to Sensualist Oshun's loft.

Mr. Rival finally made it back to Sensualist Oshun's beautiful building while expecting to spot her pretty toes at her window twinkling outside with the smell of hemp feeling the wind. He saw that her window was closed so Mr. Rival decided to grab his cream jewelry bag and walked into the building, back up the steps, and to the second floor down the hall to Sensualist Oshun's loft "118."But before he could knock, he felt her omnipresence as he stood in front of her threshold. Sensualist Oshun felt his compelling emotions at her door as she shouted out from the backroom for him to use the yellow key and just come in and get comfortable. Mr. Rival walked in as the door closed behind him; he looked around and saw that Sensualist Oshun had three candles lit across the kitchen countertop… gold, amber, and coral-colored wax beauties with flakes of gold embedded within them.

There was a copper bowl with cinnamon and honey blanketed over fresh slices of oranges with burning incents with the smell of sunflowers and hot pumpkin pie; loose peacock feathers were spreading in a trail along the floor leading him towards the sofa to sit. As he set, Sensualist Oshun walked from her back room with a mesmerizing dance in his eyes; showing the strength of her flowing power and a taste of her undying energy of love filling him with the caliber of her essence. Her rhythm is like the rivers of fierce waters sacred but in her mastered divine feminine. Mr. Rival respected her every move as she sang and danced to a slow neo-soul instrumental of meditation as the clock struck 5 pm.

Her love sparkled from her naturally oiled body as the lineation of her dance was seen through her thin kaftan holding the passage of their wishes. He adored her magnificence as not just curvy flesh but the pure mention of love itself. The virtue of her dance has placed him in a mental mirror of what he can see in his self and Sensualist Oshun; he didn't see beyond the schedule in his life through the day until now. Mr. Rival stood before her as she danced… dancing a dance of countless reasons of truly respecting her mind, her walk, and her inner prosperity. Sensualist Oshun stopped dancing and walked to the kitchen with Mr. Rival to the stove as she whispered in his ear. Then they removed each other's fabric with unbothered eyes as he placed her delectable tail on a cold stove for her to give it warmth. Her legs start opening the existence of the cosmos, in which he is not afraid of her beautiful melanin darkness. She then speaks to him slowly whispering more before he goes on a deeper journey with her once again.}

"Mr. Rival, did you handle what needed to be handled at Ms. Dulcets Jewelry Store?"

{Mr. Rival looked at Sensualist Oshun as he stood between a new purpose of her harmony, love, and ecstasy with a clear answer in mind as he spoke in a deep tone of untamed romance.}

"Sensualist Oshun, what needed to be handled at *Ms. Dulcets* will never be handled because I'd rather be in the wealth of your love boundlessly then to allow the jewels of my soul to be revived by no one but you. I only see us now and further more. Allow me to travel within you to search for the abundance of our moments, let us form something far greater than myself traveling into the chasm of your celestial body of self-luminous stars."

{Sensualist Oshun pulled him close with a smile as Mr. Rival changed the channels of her visual mind as the stove held every passionate feel of propulsion. She heals him with every thrust of what will be for them as they cook with love, using all-natural ingredients as time becomes what is real that shouldn't be explained but done or felt with time. As all eyes became closed to visualize their true awakening in the most peaceful darkness... the vastness of new love.}

"Mmmmmm... Yes!"

The Poet
B. GKL
Brotha GKL / Gawd Keenny L io' lT

STORY 2:
3:33 PM… CIGAR IN THE SHADE

STORY 2:

3:33 PM... CIGAR IN THE SHADE

Characters:
Halina and **Levi**

Today was just another day off, stuck in a time that felt like all the other calendar dates that remain shackled inside its dividing lines or boxed in. My off days always felt like a disconnected emptiness that I continued to place in my life as a reward to force myself to forget that I owned a very lucrative business. My company keeps me in conflict against the figment of time in which timing seems to always forget its damn place of who's running the measures of one's own life. My clock is selfishly naïve towards how I should determine to spend my hours of rest or exhilaration. Although, I do tend to embrace the perks of running an enterprise of perfection with trivial mishaps here, and there if not at all; when it comes to making strategic decisions, I consider myself a master of any business I choose to build.

Beyond that, I have the authority to amble from my office at any moment without ever having to provide any explanation of where or when. The greatest part of my day is to walk out of my place of business, and throw on my dark shades; commencing the bitter ferocity of my merciless engine that screamed in the mid-heart of my motorcycle when I shifted her gears. My chopper never failed me once when I needed her to let loose of all her strength beyond her point of fraction and allow me to feel the vibrations of me turning her on so she could ride me into the hanging double suns. Like always, I just flowed through traffic while my mind settled into its deep clearness. In the meantime, I soon reached the main street of lights sliding down slowly from a lemon yellow to that funky cease of burden red. I released the brakes and smoothly planted the right and left soles of my shoes onto the concrete as I stopped at the crosswalk.

As I waited for the green light while glancing down at my time piece and 3:33 pm was gazing back at me with affirmations. The numbers were locked; the lagging steel arms under the face of my watch were smooth, subtle, and performing their tocks and tics. Sitting here waiting for the change of this prolonging light truly forces the mind to think deeper; into a feature of thoughts of how the rubber of my tires has already driven me into countless miles of seeing no everlasting stops. I just can't wait to have that sea in the path of my front leather gloves guiding the success of my patience as I cut through the zephyr.

Breaking the tether of everyday living just to confide my pondering mind into the ocean; I rolled off while tightly groping the twist-grip throttle of my chopper. I was unworried about the conditions of rather or not the weather was serene or if the wind was like a chainsaw breeze across the throat. So far, today has shown no evidence of horrid rain or storms trying to decide my options by turning me away from my moment of boundless tranquility. I never let anything sway my need to unwind alongside the shoreline; as the crashing body of water gently guides my words to speak from my secluded thoughts into the surge of aquatic coast as it listens to me as my tongue rambles.

I just enjoy watching the sunshine gleam upon the motion of ravaging waters leaping over its ripples of incomprehensible mysteries, twisting around unsolved and calling forth to all eyes when one is near. As the two suns just hang above the ocean like two chandeliers with candles burning in the air. There is nothing like a day of equanimity when your mind is overflowing under the chafe of stress; but no matter what, I always stay in tune with the centerpiece of peaceful surroundings presenting its piquant calmness.

After brainstorming down the road I finally arrived offshore, I walked across the timber bridge stretching its distance from the parking lot to the sand. It's a blistering hot walk across a painted red velvet structure of color chipping off the bridge side into natures peeking weeds, grass, and large mounds like the dunes of Egypt. The structure timber towered over the deep humps of sand that led all that came towards the ocean bellowing to the sky like wolves towards the crescent star as the sea holds a full belly of fins. As I walked across nearing the bridge end to the beach with only one focus… to relax. I began rolling up the legs of my pants; I started to remove the confinement of my shoes to discharge my nerves so that my feet could heal in the sun's hot sand.

I love the natural stepping feel to cleanse me with its electric charge from within and throughout every tissue of muscle that I am. As I humbly acknowledge the push of wind as the sea brushes the sand from my toes and around my shins. I stood within the vicinity of the ocean of movement to comprehend the sharp rigid touch of small broken shells somewhat jabbing my bottom feet. The sea foam of the ocean pushed upon the beating blood vessels of my ankles. I decided to pull my shirt from my flesh throwing it flat to the land along with my shoes to grasp the ambiance upon my skin; I was taking in the view before me, near my favorite location. I set down on top of my shirt with my feet pressed in *Gaia's* bed of sand. At this moment, I paid no attention to anything but the pure nirvana that mellows me out; I guess I could deviate from my focus if the alteration is worth me changing my focal point of nature's imposing wrath.

My thoughts were sunnily interrupted when I overheard a familiar sound of zipper steel grinding against itself. It was heard over the crisp noise of the moving depths of the sea as I looked over toward the distraction. The sight of her satin-like shoulders, and the pose of her carelessness as she ignores all that walked near her relaxation. I valued her presence while my eyes could not help but admire her without disturbing her lonesome peace. My ears honored the clean-cutting sound that came from this woman's fine cigar being sliced inward as she decapitated the foot of its unlit **Foot** and **Filler**. After the observance of her in my shades, I then continued to appreciate the earthy matt brown of her lip rouge moistening the head cap of its wrap. She rotated the ending above the scorching blaze upon the tuck end of her super premium pyramid cigar like a true gentlewoman of divine regard.

My eyes were paralyzed with her classy gestures taunting me by the seaside as she began sliding down the gold-bearing band of her perfectly humidified cigar and dropping the ring on its bottom after a couple of long puffs to the atmosphere. She proceeded to ignore humanity as strangers briefly passed by with a starved gaze trying to relate to her radiance as she set comfortably near the salty wet living art of sea. The waters just washed over every curvy portion of her naturalness sitting close to the consistency of ocean coming and going.

As I set, I was unable to look away as my eyes became swallowed by her ethereal splendor; I saw nothing but the sea and the joy upon her from the dark frames of my sunglasses. I watched the smoke drift from the open volcano of her considerable yielding lips just holding the cloud in the roof of her mouth; the vapors coated her taste buds like a hot tub steaming out on a deck of winter. The smoke begins to pour from her chamber like a blown-out candle in a room of ceiling fans set on low, pushing the smoke around the openness of her beautiful white teeth. I watched her completely rejoice and it made me not want to disturb the splendid time of this loner's peace but yet, distantly, I truly respected her moment. She then leaned back against the sand a bit, allowing the two suns in the sky to get a taste of her as she puffed her sweet cigar.

This high-spirited woman just set in her elegance with a black tailored swim suit that confined her plump diamond hips. She then flicks the ash of the cigar on to the shore letting the wind take it to sea. In my eyes, all this woman was missing was me drizzling dessert wine upon her hamstrings and letting the pearl drips bead down her legs to only fall from her knees on to my chops as I lay beneath her harmony. I then had hoped to express the mood she was placing me in from just me not being able to turn my shades away from this distant opportunity. I can only contemplate what the unity is between her and what her name might be; I'm curious, I wonder if her name matches her hazelnut-brown body sun gazing under the heat with her sweet-smelling cigar fumes twisting towards my inhale and over the aggressive ocean of clashing ripples.

As a business man, my motion of action towards anything uncommon that pulls at my interest this much is worth taking a risk of shooting my shot. Even if it's a moment of me getting rejected or an unexpected contentment of my goal reaching something more than adequate in my eyes; this may be a difficult task but yet the type of woman that maybe worth any outcome of how she reacts to me. I assume she would be a woman who's not unhinged but unbothered and independently unamused by simple measures to gain her time by a foreseeable approach. She looks like a lady that one has to earn a moment to converse with, definitely while she is centered in her peaceful space on this shore. Before I decided to look away from her, she leaned to the left, and let her cigar rest on a small hump of sand next to her towel and hips. The cigar continued to burn while the wind blew on the settled ash and reddened its ember-like tip.

I gazed at her once more as she looked entirely soul-equipped for everything I was hoping to gain once I decided to stand and succeed. Respectfully, I was determined not to be ignored so easily by the wrath of her comfort as she relaxed in a mode of self-love. So, she then decided to close her eyes and lay flat on her towel under the oven of dual suns seizing her skin with its rays. As the heat wrapped the gift of her body's poetic form of speechless words in my head… damn. I jolt forward placing my right hand in the scorching sand to rise above the imprint of where I set. I stood as I picked up my shirt to brush the sand from my legs. With my side-eye from behind my dark shades, I held the blurred side image of her lying as one with the tropical setting before us. I looked at both suns flaring in the sky like two great counterparts birthed from the soul of two phoenix birds looking for a way to infinitely ignite. But, to waste no more of time's illusion to run things, I picked up my shoes and began walking her way. As I walked towards her, I wondered, how could one just lay so at ease in the brightness of the sky without sunglasses to bear the radiance that sweeps across this blistering land.

I scanned every part of her with goodwill as I got closure with profound questions in my soul about this woman here. I stood about a car length from where she stretched out in relaxation with her right ankle crossing the left leg and both her hands clinched across her waist. Her soft hands barely covered the tattooed head of Anubis peeking from under her black tailored swim suit; I wondered if the full tattoo of Anubis covered her full *Yoni*... such thoughts are hard to ignore. I just love a closed-book woman with an oddness of something concealed about her presence yet to be truly discovered.

Within seconds of being near this gentlewoman, I felt awakened by any woman with some kind of lovely love handles... rather she was large, curvy, medium, or slender; a soft stomach pudge or fit but in my eyes, I just love the essence of a powerful woman with a warm heart. One might assume that I have a slight belly fetish among all women of all sizes as long as she has a strong mind. The natural bezel of her lashes is like a keen cutting tool ripping through the force of my actions on edge.

Standing near her, my feet imbedded deeper into the sand as I lingered about, hesitant, trying not to become a walking contradiction towards the confident man that I have worked hard to become. So, I unburied my feet with the sea crashing against the shore loudly beside me like an audience swaying back and forth screaming from the stands... waves rushing me to speak my peace. The sweet smell of her cigar became more powerful in the current of air, and the sweating of her skin gleamed from the ray of light. She made me feel like an apparition intruding upon inviolable grounds. Before my shadow could reach the edge of her beach towel, with her eyes closed she immediately spoke with facts and no threats.

"I recommend that you stop there; I rather you not continue to walk any further towards the spot that I temporally own at the moment please think wisely. I do over stand that this is a public beach, and all that come here are welcome because of the beach's naive rules but I am not a part of the beach. I come here often with hopes to clear my mind, and I do not wish to be rude to you or insensitive but if you choose to go against my kind warning… there is a 500 S&W Magnum near me unseen. Strangers keep wanting to bother me, and also tend to linger about as you are now; so, now that you have heard my issue, peace, and my mental reason. What is it that I can help you with so that I may continue with my day?"

I stood fascinated by her pure rawness, holding my shoes in one hand with my shirt tucked in my back pocket hanging loose in the wind with sand still falling from it while feeling a bit salty about her quick brutal response. I dropped my shoes next to where I stood, and slowly placed both my hands down in my front pockets with my thumbs hanging out to express high confidence in my body language regardless of whether she was on the defense towards me or not. Because I am an owner of my own business, I inner stood that one can never be to alert when dealing with strangers so I respected her caution and didn't take it too personally.

Yet, I decided to master a different approach in my mind to answer her properly before she abruptly decided to reach for the *500 S&W Magnum* that she claimed to have. I took my hand from my right pocket, removed my shades, and let them fall where my shoes set. I then spoke from a side of myself that shies behind my spontaneous ego. I figured if a woman of this caliber could keep me unfocused this long, then why not speak to her from an unpredictable point of view? I then spoke to her with the goal of getting her eyes to open as she sun-gazed waiting for my response.

"Well ma'am, at this point, does it even matter what you might be able to help with? I am a slumberous highbrowed man who had to motivate his self to walk over to you. I accepted all consequences, positive or negative once I approached you from where I set. I didn't care if our brief encounter turned out to be

horrible or a moment captivating the here and now. I came to these salty serene waters for the same purpose as you stated; I am also here for elation under the two suns above, and this sea of unsolved history that does not care to be bothered without love. Miss, know that I usually only speak this much when I am handling business but poetically rambling is a bad old habit of mine in which I have kept hidden until now. You seem to be someone that inspires my speech to become what it was... something lost in the depth and narrating love riddles from the marrow."

After I spoke, she remained stretched out on her beach towel with her right ankle crossing her left leg and her hands across her waistline. Her left hand came up to her arched eyebrows to give her eyes some shade as she squinted up at me to catch a glimpse of a man who spoke with such deep roots beneath his voice. As she looked up at me, I was staring off into the intimate tides of talking waves motivating my openness. She then spoke as she set up to retrieve a different flavor of smoke; She pulled a Grande cigar from her portable red leather cigar case and prepped it as she spoke to me as I stood waiting to hear her speak once more.

"Well, before you catch a cramp in your legs just standing there! I need to hear you speak your name before I bestow my own. I need to be comfortable with you before inviting you to sit down with me on my favorite beach towel. Don't forget if this gets weird after the name exchange just know that this lovely one always stays ready with a brown polished trigger finger that's been restless. So, my kind and deep verbalizer, what is your name?"

I looked down at her laughing but I remained composed as she puffed her cigar smiling with one eyebrow raised. Then the vapors of her puff rolled out from the corner of her lips to the side of her mellow mocha cheekbones. Smoke rolled out from beneath all sides of her purple Wide Brim Big Bowknot Straw Hat and her black linen head scarf. I then stroked my moustache down to my chin of hairs; I watched her look at me reading my posture and body language while I was readying my mind to answer her question.

"Well miss, my father and mother named me *Levi*, they both

41

wanted a name that motivates me to remain a strong harmonious man that never forgets to be joined with my roots of where I came from; basically, I was created by two damn poets that loved the deepness of life."

For some reason, we both just instantly shared a quick laugh and she held her smooth cigar off to the side while smirking at me as she talked with a bit more ease.

"So… LEVI! That name would have been a hard guess if I had to assume but it truly fits you well and I like the way it sounds when it's spoken in your tone. Furthermore Levi, my folks named me Halina, they were country people who moved to the islands before I was born; we survived mostly off the vegetation and fruit of the land while living in a nice orange shack. I loved growing up by the calm serene seas feeling the rays of the two suns of light shining on my skin as I set in the garden for hours after school. I loved smelling my mom's perfume from the shack after she would leave to make her runs to the mart for extra things needed for supper. I can also smell the memories of my papa's cigar burning in the wind as he stood at the grill cooking fresh salmon and Mahi-mahi feeling the yard with the scent of fulfillment.

My apologies Levi, maybe it's something about your presence that makes a woman like me express her mind's bliss from the past. As you can see my towel is large enough to seat us both without any discomfort, please sit next to me at let's see how long you can last in much deeper conversation."

I looked at her with a slick grin while leaving my shoes and shades where they were and set down next to *Halina* to grasp the view that made her love this shore as much as I did. As she puffed her stick in a peaceful silence the beach gradually became empty around us with only the sounds of the seaside, and nature's elements making music as the creatures blended into its wholeness. I decided to break my silence.

"Halina, as we sit here, I need you to know that I hope to gain nothing but what I have already received in the brief memories we design. I can tell that you are a true realistic woman with much more to know of then what pulled me through a sandy stroll next

42

to you."

Halina looked at me and placed her cigar on the same hump of sand at her left side by the first cigar that no longer holds that lingering heat. She then reached into her straw tote beach bag that was set between us; with her right hand, she pulled out a fresh bottle of Caribbean Rum and she looked at me as her eyes talked that talk. I looked at *Halina* while in my moment of feeling perplexed but yet wondering what her motive was as her mellow voice articulated her philosophy of certain matters.

"Respect this bottle of Caribbean Rum that I hold in my grip as I offer a portion of this good drink to the sand for all that as transitioned, and for all new things to come into renewal. Levi, you walked over to me and placed your ego to the side to be upfront with me. I foresee that, I felt that from you as you stood calmly opening up to me. A strong melanin man or any man that can be rational should be appreciated; you all should be complimented for stepping out from the state of self-norm to powerfully relieve one's self of all clichés of existence. I get allot of foolish men trying to approach me in vulgar ways, absurdity, with nothing more than an overused third leg trying to moisten my Barrita Orchid with the bait of affluence. I am not a harlot; I am a 56-year-old woman patiently waiting to be romanced with sincerity, not ignorance. With all that being said… Levi, allow me to pour some of my delectable rum for a man like yourself, and rarities of men that speak from a different flavor of real outspoken gate keepers with the keys to a fed-up woman's interest."

I looked at *Halina* respectfully admiring every word channeled towards me from the softness of her lips; I never heard too many women speak in such a heartfelt manner as she had. So, I insinuated yes in agreeance with my eyes toward her kind gesture as she grabbed a palm full of sand with her left hand and turned her fist around and out as she opened her fingers. Within her grasping control, *Halina* then poured a bit of rum over the earth shore; you can then smell the strong aroma of overripe bananas and pineapples as the rum pours. I watched the suspension of brown passion and the sand became unified as one in a thickness of earthly clumps falling from *Halina's* hand. Over us, the two-blistering suns in the sky flaunted their temperamental rays of scorching light food feeding the flesh of all beneath the shine. As we set, I looked at her as she used part of the beach towel to clean her hand of Caribbean Rum and shore land as she retrieved her cigar from the sand. I then let my words fall into her ears.

"Halina, **I'm a 51-year-old man in search of contentment and the authenticity of every breath I take. While giving more meaning other than just letting go, only to take in another breath without giving it worth, other than just having the power to. What I'm saying to you is that, to me, life is bigger than just prevailing but inhaling the gasp of air after taking risks in life without the fairytale of fear. To me, Life is a choice, and death is not an option even beyond the transition. My business is thriving, and I have so many people who depend on me to keep the lucrative gates of my company open for wealth; I sit in my office at times just overhearing the frivolous needs of those who work for me.**

They are wonderful people but have an unfulfilling appetite for more, and more; they seem to keep fishing too deep in an ocean for satisfaction, and fulfillment while having a full bucket of fine catch on the boat. With them, it's all about the curiosity of what else could they attain, instead of honoring what they have already gained! I love what I have built but in my free time nothing exists but me, my motorcycle being the curvy chopper that it is with the natural scent of earth going through my nose as I ride."

Halina then rested her right hand across her stomach on to her left side. She alluringly puffed her cigar with her index curving down, firmly pressed against her thumb as the body of her cigar lounged upon the top flesh of her middle-left finger. *Halina* had this feel about her that made me feel as if she was listening to me with more than just her ears but yet with the soulful entirety of insight as she just listened to me ramble. While relaxing, I felt like the dual suns were now wielding my strong will to be unattached from this simulated world; along with *Halina's* natural ability to create infinite bliss wherever she dwells. Is this supposed to be one powerful moment or a life of moments driven by a power full of potential love? Furthermore, we stop talking to value the peace that we both came for… the ocean!

The motion of the sea was like a stirred Resin of Blue Tropical colors mixing and spreading out like Epoxy poured off to the confines of which it swallows whole. The spiritual speech of this vast body of water teaches one to yield before it and know it as one that heals, destroys, and is something that is an unfathomable inner space. *Halina* then spoke to me, taking a half puff of her cigar.

"Levi, I know that we don't know one another but my parents raised me to always speak my mind with a sense of boundaries; just here me out, I think about certain life questions every day. We sit on this shore taking in all that we taste, see, feel, and hear while holding on to all that we have gained in this life… from all aspects. We as people have yet to reach the peak of what is towards mattering at all; we learn, rise, fall, heal, destroy, fight, and mature just to start where we begin… LEARNING! I am also sick of being food for something I don't over stand or have ever seen, just draining all of us of our energy; sometimes I feel like a prisoner to the thought of life and death without the sight to see my constraints holding me in between at my scarred knees. At this point, I just want to make the best of what I think is important to me until it's all over."

"Halina, I believe that you are speaking of something that crosses the mind of many; most of us lie to ourselves to remain stuck with what's wrongly done to us, and force it to feel right. We come out of the womb into the dense poison made for us to survive in. *Halina,* I have learned to do as I please as long as it makes sense, I have done allot of shit in my life, things that only hurt me in the end. I protected others but destroy myself with the obsession for wealth but I no longer give a damn about that; I guess I want to be free from all of it, just like you. *Levi Denmarc* is who I am, I'm from *The Denmarc Bloodline,* and my family is not to be played with or taken as a joke in any type of way, trust me. That is all I can say about that. I chose to stay out of the way as much as possible and create a positive way of living instead of what I knew of alongside my deadly relatives. For now, it's just me and my motorcycle… free and study; my business is just a necessary force to help all that work for me to relinquish any negative karma. I embrace my imperfections until it's all over."**

"Well okay Levi, I love a man with mystique and one that's willing to face his self, I can respect that. Hay look, how about we continue

this conversation on your chopper, and grab a bite to eat; I grabbed an Uber here today anyhow, I can't stand driving my car half the time because I'm used to riding horses from where am from. That's if you are not scared of a woman that's carrying… ha-ha."

"Ha-ha okay *Halina,* I can see that you also have a dark sense of humor, I like that in a woman. We can do that; it's no problem sense I make my own rules in my place of business. Also, I have the perfect place we can eat in which I believe you would love but you may want to change your clothes before we ride out!"

"Relax Levi, A true woman of deep thought always thinks ahead; I always keep a beach locker here for emergencies. I will gather my things, and meet you in the parking lot with your chopper and ready to go, I will only be a moment… okay? Also don't assume I would leave you hanging, I'd rather stand you up but that's neither nor there. See you in the parking lot!"

We then stood to are feet grabbing our things to head out. While walking away I couldn't help but get a look back at *Halina's* build of beauty. Her damn timing was on point because she was already looking at me; we both bust out laughing as we then walked a moment of separate ways. Nowadays it's hard to get a deep conversation with meaning, and now I get it from this snappy piece of loveliness. I was looking forward to this outing. On the way out I knew that I wasn't returning to my office at all for today. When I got to my chopper and took a seat on the leather curve of my chopper's middle dip waiting for *Halina.* I then sent a text to the proprietor of my favorite high-end private cigar spot to set the VIP so that we could continue our conversation in peace. While waiting on *Halina,* I felt the warm breath of the ocean rush out into the parking lot against my body; it was a calm push to let me know the breeze was always with me.

As I sat on my chopper I leaned to my right and turned on some of that smooth soulful jazz. Soon after, on the left side of my view, as the jazzing jams caressed my choppers speakers, *Halina's* foxy ass came across the chipping bridge of flaking paint. She had that setting a car on fire and waiting to exhale type of walk. *Halina* was rocking this Violet and White Loose Ruffle Neck Pleated Wide Leg Cami Jumpsuit… fitting just right. I watched the same breeze I felt combing

46

its windy fingers through **Halina's** Short Two-Tone Curls and around her Tapered back and sides cut, and lined. I find that a woman who humbly admires every inch of her appearance. A **Kween** that's versatile switching from a laid-back chill to a real classy vibe; that shit just swings my pulse into a Newton's cradle of clashes, the signature of love for self truly hardens my stance on not ruining this opportunity. As she walked towards me in her T-strap Flat Sandals with genuine diamonds shining on top of the straps; the diamonds led from her ankle to the inner spaces of her toes as the gold thong of her flats relaxed against her soft skin. **Halina** then stopped near me admiring my chopper's build and my choice of jazz spilling smooth jelly from my speakers of sweet serenades.

As she walks around my ride, bouncing her shoulders up and down with her hips shifting forward; her top lip folded over her bottom lip as she recognizes the funky soulful jazz of J. Bradshaw. I then looked over to her as I grabbed my helmet to give to her, I only had one, this was a moment unprepared for but it was all good. She then looked at me with a laugh followed by her pungent nature with words.

"What would I need with a helmet Levi? Just feel what I have to say, I am no fool to safety but I rather you show me how secure I should be with me just holding on to your body. If I am protected by unknown energies beyond this multi-shaped world then I won't be harmed whether I am doing foolish things or not. You must over stand Levi, I bareback horses unclothed in The Amazon rainforest every other year just for the hell of it.

So, know that you don't have to worry about me. Just guide your focus more towards discovering my certitude. Also, fear of anything is something I wish to always conquer head-on as much as I can in this life full of escapades to endure. Just keep this in mind, I trust that you will be the same gentlemen I set with on this beach, and if you decide to be the opposite of that which you have shown it is going to be a problem well handled. So, let me sit in front of you while facing you as you control this ride but mind yourself Levi, and don't hold back on the acceleration."

All I could do is look at **Halina** standing on the other side of my chopper talking that sexy saucy shit I love in a presumptuous woman.

I felt no need to be difficult against a woman who seems to be the type of lady who's on the fearless side of life, but I had thought in my head that she seemed to be holding on to just the perimeters of life itself. I then stood up placing my helmet on my thoughts, and swung my right leg over my chopper to be seated while stating my quick thoughts to **Halina.**

"Look here ladylove, for some reason every time I hear you speak from such a courageous depth, I feel some sort of fight in you, something that's being guided to a poetic ending. Maybe it's just me being extra, and reaching a bit far with what I feel but let's just make this move... let's enjoy this day like our last. I will wear my helmet to protect us both if the worst were to happen, just know, you will have my body as cover but just hold me tight."

After I spoke, **Halina** looked back at the ocean with this constrained tear sitting in the circle colors of her eyes; she then fluttered her eyelids to suppress the emotional waters. I didn't want **Halina's** mood to be ignored, so I grabbed a short leather mat from my chopper's saddlebag and placed it over my gas tank for her to sit comfortably. I then reached out to her with my right hand in silence to insinuate that it was all good, no judgment, and that I inner stood. She quietly gave me her left hand as I took a stand over my chopper, feet firm on both sides; I then grasped her waist placing her in the erotic Upstanding Citizen position.

I sat down slowly and placed my hands over her shoulders to take hold of my hand grips; as I kicked back the jiffy stand and centered my ride from its chilled parked lean. **Halina** pulled up her Wide Leg Cami Jumpsuit over her knees as her thighs rested on top of my own. Her legs and feet hang by the sides of my lower limbs and my chopper exhaust pipes. As **Halina's** arms wrapped around my chest with her hands meeting her soft wrist as they locked at my spine; she laid her left ear against my shoulder over the pounding balanced tempo of my heart. Her full-bosomed chest vigorously pressed hard upon my cage of muscle and ribs starching and stable.

The scent of Smooth Rum with a hint of Bulgarian White Rose and a Delicious Brazilian Amber and Night Blooming Jasmine flowed from her body and printed onto all that she touched upon me. **Halina** was greater than what the word different could convey, her personality was like pure Agave Nectar poured over gunpowder and ancient scrolls of wisdom. I then felt the warmth of her tears steeping through my shirt. So, I turned up the radio with some of that *Computer Love* and slid my keys into the warm cavity of my hog… starting up my chopper's sexy noise. I sped out of the beach parking lot onto the road and down the ramp to the expressway to merge into the lightness of traffic. I was doing 83 mph, clean; *Halina* was holding me tight without her head ever leaving my body. Her seated position never hindered my skill to handle my machine as one should do with strength, balance, and control. Driving as fast as I was, I wasn't worried about the law not once, because I knew that being from *The Denmarc Bloodline* held high regard and that I was considered off-limits by any law enforcement.

When I ride, I'm never ridiculous with breaking too many laws but selective depending upon how important it is for me to be somewhere. With being known, today was hella important to be free from all things outside this moment with *Halina.* Furthermore, I turned a 33-minute drive into a 21-minute ride on the express. Nevertheless, it was time for me to slow it down and come up the ramp to the uptown city streets of high buildings, open roads, and people driving with a purpose. As we set at the light I could see the location of the high-end private cigar spot. Then the relaxed breathing of *Halina's* bust gave me the feeling that she was surly asleep but aware of her surroundings upon the tight grip she held, I was surprised that she never let go of me, not even once.

I felt that I should wake her but before I could give her that deep whisper of disturbance the light turned green, so I decided to just wait until we arrived at the smoke joint. I then made the left turn and headed to the private cigar spot within my sight. Once we reached the Luxury Iron Gates of my destination I placed my left palm on the Biometric Scanner. Once my identity was quickly verified the iron gates opened without hesitation. As I drove through while *Halina* remained rested as the Luxury Iron Gates shut behind us as I drove into my reserved parking space ahead.

I always respected this place for its classy benevolence for its members. This cigar spot has that unbothered comfort of those who have limited drive for elevation or the smoking wisdom to make it behind these Luxury Iron Gates. The waiting list here is as long as the time it takes for one soul to smoke a box of premium cigars. Those who wish to be part of this clandestine movement have a past that's charred and covered in somber smoke. For those that know deeply the true name of this place… which is the *"I'Am'All-Cigar Spot"*, where the real *Cigar Herfs* are held with many great minds, and cultures to converse many topics of disaster, lessons, and success. After most of my excessive thoughts subsided to the back of my mind, I leaned my chopper onto its jiffy stand with my key turning my ride off, and onto a left-leaning rest. I nudged my chest forward to get *Halina* to rise from the catnapping hold she had on my body.

She began to lift her head with a smile of harmony and a sight of eyes blazing with the liveness of a hidden renegade. As she smiled beneath the shade of my head and my body's shadow; her swaying legs dangled at my left and right side. Proportions of her warm spread set perfectly on the matt of leather that she set upon; *Halina's* hazelnut-brown pillow plumpness separated deeper to the cleft of her inner line. The leather matt protected her bottom quake of goods, protecting her from the heat of my chopper's tank of premium patrol while its liquids patiently regained its lukewarm composure in time.

"So, *Halina*, did I make you feel secure? Because of the way you were sleeping mid-ride, I assume I handled my part adequately. My chopper is not as wild as your bareback riding a horse naked on mother nature's beautiful body of land but my machine has its own risk of excitement to bring to your thrill-seeking spirit… You Dig!"

"Well Levi, don't get a big head over a ride, OK? Just because I challenged you to protect me does not mean you were required to accept my teasing; just consider this a curiosity of kindness towards the completion of your actions. Anyways, would you mind helping a lady off of your chopper and firm thighs so that I can stretch my legs while you give a woman some brief info on the place that you drove us to!"

After her words ceased, I gradually rose with her legs over my thighs like two dainty hazelnut-brown silk ribbons waiting to enhance the ground with her touch of seduce. While securely holding *Halina*, I immediately stepped my right foot over my chopper to its left side onto the concrete; I released my hold as she slowly did the same. I felt the warmness of her hamstrings sliding down my legs with the front of her T-strap Flat Sandals bejeweled with genuine diamonds meeting at the front of my shoes. At this point, both of our arms were placed down at our sides with us holding in enough intimate desire between us to overfill books of romantic rage. *Halina* then placed her hands at the sides of my *Silver Chrome Half Helmet* and unleashed my chin strap; she then lifted the helmet from my crest and placed it down on my chopper's seat. *Halina* then gave me some more of her slick sexy words as they slid out her mouth like a *Chocolate Schlong Sickle Candy Sucker...* sicky-like.

"Now, Mr. Levi, would you mind answering my questions about where we are and is the food as tasty as the way you eat me up with your puzzling mind? I can see how you poetically pause within your mannerisms and tone in front of me. Humbly, I know that I am an attractive woman but you look at me beyond all of that Levi; I know you do because I can relate by the way I am with you now but anyhow, talk to me handsome."

"*Halina*, you are a pistol! I respect the forwardness that you keep throwing at me the way that you fluently do; that's a habit that many don't carry within these times. Furthermore, I picked this place on behalf of something we both have in common; I was intrigued by the respect, class, and passion that you have for the art of smoking cigars. The sensual way that you handled your cigar back at the beach was like watching an intimate moment at a stage play while spectators waited for the last line of your blown smoke to cheer. So, I made special arrangements for us to be here, I figured that you would love it; this place is called the *"I'Am'All-Cigar Spot"*. The Denmarc Bloodline is well known and respected here for being the earth and water to its roots of where it began.

The superior rank of my ancestors is the essence of the *"I'Am'All"* movement before it became many structures that represent its name. *The* name *"I'Am'All"* is used to carry countless businesses under its core command. Just like the building we stand before today... which is the *"I'Am'All-Cigar Spot."* Beyond the short history lesson, this place is well known for the best cigars, top

firewater, food, and baked goods straight from *Lil' Miss Tasty Cakes,* which is our family bakery. It's a lot to uncover on what all goes down here but let's head in so we can chat a bit deeper."

"Levi, I guess you are unselfish towards satisfying my comfort in the process of your peace… that's a nice quality to have as well; So, feel free to guide the way and lead us into your place of relief and ambiance of unbiased smoke."

I smirked and walked forward to stand beside **Halina** while bending my elbow out to her; we then walked arm in arm-to get things started. As we walked under the blue, and gold long entrance canopy leading towards the entry upon the Red Oak Wood Double Doors of the *"I'Am'All-Cigar Spot."* As we stood at the double doors, we both paused for a moment and inhaled deeply at the same time taking in the smell of rich and complex aromas; that lavish scent of cigars seeping from the door's red oaks wooden lining.

We took in the pungency of the lit cigar's release of earthy tones, cedar, leather, spice, coffee, and a slight sweetness on top of fresh notes of cut leather. Nevertheless, we had that smirk of damn right upon our faces. I then opened one of the doors as I gestured **Halina** to head in first as we both felt that sweet wind of wealth in the air. There's nothing wealthier than watching **Halina** walking in front of me filling my path behind her with the unforgettable fragrance of her endearing aura. Her Violet and White Loose Ruffle Neck Pleated Wide Leg Cami Jumpsuit unburied the sensuous side of my mind with the way that she swayed her hips without trying to swing it to my leer. **Halina's** Short Two-Tone Curls and Tapered back and sides made me want to lick the spine of her neck.

Beyond all of that, as we walked further, we passed the proprietor's chocolate Cocker Spaniel relaxing near the front entry by the coat check area. He was wolfing down a steak with yams out of a wooden bowl. His name tag glistened with the words **Chew'Bacca aka Bacca Baby** upon it; **Halina** couldn't help but reach down to stroke the chocolate curls of his wavy mohawked hairstyle. We then carried on with our walk toward our reserved seats while being greeted graciously by those sipping, puffing, and unwinding. As we walked past cigars lifting and laying upon trays of ash; liquor being served to empty hands or a pour becoming more of a slow stream into a vacant glass. The herbal notes of lemongrass flowed from the chef's kitchen from ahead; as servers came and went into the swinging doors of meals prepared beyond them. While in motion a uniformed gentleman respectfully intervened with our path while walking us further on to our reserved area as he spoke.

"Hello *Mr. Denmarc* and Madame, my name is *De'troit*, and I will be guiding you the rest of the way. *Mr. Denmarc* I must tell you that we have upgraded your VIP to our VVIP room, and we hope that you and the Madame enjoy the tasteful feel of our newly designed smoking area upstairs. Walk with me please!"

I nodded my head towards *De'troit* to proceed, as we followed *Halina* looked back at me and whispered with that mood of arousal coy, and that hard-to-get tone within her voice, *"Don't be a showoff, Levi... Haha, ok... MR. DENMARC... HAHA."* I just responded with a smirk while she talked a little shit with her seductive chuckling with a body and mind that could make wealth feel powerless and cheaply made. As *De'troit* walked us to our upgrade, leading us upstairs to a short hallway that had no doors or windows; there was a very large aquarium in the middle of this short distance hallway. This massive aquarium was filled with multiple Lionfish just swimming about in a blissful cadence. *Halina* and I stood there confused at *De'troit* because for myself, I come here often and this was an all-new setup for me and an odd place to be taken to. *De'troit* then smiled as he walked away back to the steps to leave as he spoke to us on the way down.

"*Mr. Denmarc* and Madame, this is the furthest that I am allowed to take you but please do not look so confused, just walk forward to feed the Lionfish. You will soon over stand what truly awaits you; don't be fooled by what you see before you. Enjoy your stay."

As *De'troit* left us, we both glanced at one another in a strange manner while walking slowly to figure out what this was about. At this point, both of our stomachs were growling with hunger with every step forward in a fashion of curious shuffles towards what felt like a strange paradox. Reaching the middle of this short hallway we turned to our left in front of the massive aquarium of beautiful yet venomous Lionfish swimming about. As we stared at this aquatic hold of stones of life and lights showcasing the elegance it keeps. *Halina* then noticed an orange button on the right bottom side with the words *"Fish Feed"* written on it. *Halina* slowly bends over and down to its press and I'll be damn if the Lionfish didn't become Insignificant in that short moment as I looked over at her.

Halina's Cami Jumpsuit hugged her by the back, between, center, and forward to the point I swear her *Yoni* blew me a kiss as she pressed the orange button and stood back up ever so sultrily. She then positioned herself close to me as the massive aquarium made strange noises. Then a bunch of live *Yellowtail Snapper Fish* flowed into the water of *Lionfish* to be suddenly eaten. As the *Lionfish* moved aggressively in its waters, the movement in the tank triggered a wide staircase to come down slowly from above us on our right side; as the staircase came down the massive aquarium moved back into the wall behind its location.

Halina and I stepped back as the staircase became level with the floor on the right side of us; as we looked up, we could see the flickering hot brewing lights. As the lights flared, we got an irresistible whiff of Cedarwood from above, we then looked at one another and began walking up the staircase to waste no more time. Once we reached the top, we stood in a **Circular Cedarwood Room** that had a cast iron fireplace that was built around the entire room of its central cedar walls. As the fireplace burned around this circled work of art, we embraced the room's balanced temperature and all that was waiting for us.

There was a **Cigar Brown Leather Curved Sofa** with a long **Charcoal Stone** colored **Quarry Coffee Table** in front of it. This table had a brown Humidor with a glass top revealing the cedar wood and premium *I'Am'All Cigars* waiting for their flavors to be discovered. The Coffee table also had one large **Marble Cigar Ashtray**, one torch lighter, and two empty glasses to persuade a thrill. This room hits the mind with so much sexy creativity; from the metal rack of liquor mounted to the wall of cedar panels and the chandelier fixture of twisted cast Iron shining down its erotic dim lights. *Halina* and I were amazed and damn sure turned on by the room just being as perplexed as it was. We just continued forward to the sofa to finally be seated and then the voice of *De'troit* was heard from the phone on the metal rack of liquor.

"Hello again *Mr. Denmarc* and Madame. I will make this brief before we leave you both completely to enjoy the privacy of the VVIP room. For you *Mr. Denmarc* we have your favorite vegetarian dish being prepared and Madame, is there anything special that you would like our chef to create for you tonight."

"Well, hello again Mr. De'troit, if it's okay with you I would like to have what Levi is having because what a man loves to eat frequently can tell a lot about who he is from another aspect. But that is neither nor there, would you please make sure there are no peanuts of any kind in my dish because I am highly allergic? Also Mr. De'troit, please just call me Halina!"

"Wonderful Madame, that will not be a problem, *Ms. Halina. Mr. Denmarc's* favorite dish is a well-known recipe that originated in Africa, it is a "Red-Red Bean Stew" with a side of Fried Plantains; for dessert is the puff-puff doughnuts. Does that sound palatable to you *Ms. Halina?"*

"Ooooh... Yes, that sounds lovely Mr. De'troit, thank you."

After 15 minutes or so, our food was served to us by the chef personally along with 1 waiter; she came up to us in her spotless chef attire with the 1 waiter walking behind her with our food. They greeted us briefly and set our food down on the **Quarry Coffee Table** in front of us; they then left quickly to allow us to enjoy her work of art in peace as the waiter closed the staircase behind him and the chef as they left down and out. After an hour of stimulating conversation, exquisite food, and flirtatious cues... it was time for myself and *Halina* to pour up, smoke a little, and enjoy the cast iron of fire that burned around us.

I stood up and headed to the metal rack and picked out some rum as I held it up to see if *Halina* was feeling my drink of choice. She then agreed with a subtle shimmy of her shoulders and we both smirked as I checked out the rest of the spirits that set upon the metal rack. While I lingered a bit *Halina* began prepping the cigars for us with a clean cut or two before we put some heat to the foot of our cigar blends; I didn't mind this elegant woman reading my stick the way she does it so proficiently. Before leaving the metal rack of spirits I connected my phone's Bluetooth to the speaker once I noticed it. I turned on a hip-hop jazz instrumental, the tone was funky, dark, and passionate at the same time. I began walking back to the sofa with the bottle of Rum and sat down slowly to pour the Rum into our empty glasses. Within seconds of the slow falling pour, we began to light our cigars at the same time as we sat back on the sofa puffing and clicking glasses and then things went a bit south. As *Halina* looked around the room at all its exquisiteness and bluntly gave me her words straight up with no chaser.

"Levi, you remember what I said to Mr. De'troit… about the part about being able to tell a lot about a man just off of how and what he eats. You have culture and precision, and you're bold, dependable yet ruined by so much betrayal but not broken. Your choice of meal has so much going on but it makes sense once someone takes the time to enjoy the fulfilment of it. Your heart is compassionate and I would love to know it further; what I am trying to say is that I wish that I had run into you years ago before I was diagnosed with a rare and deadly heart disease. My doctor gave me the news in February and I was told that I would not make it to December of this year. Levi, I just want you to continue to be romantic as you are, and make love to me as if our lovemaking had unbreakable vows… just take my mind away from it all, for a moment."

Hearing that come out of *Halina's* mouth didn't sadden the mood but yet gave me clarity on how she was at the beach, the tears she shed on my chopper up to now. She has everything that a good man could ask for but was given such life-shaking news. I then set everything down placing my hands upon her feet, and begin removing her sandals of diamonds as I genuinely begin respecting her wishes. I took her drink and cigar from her hold and placed them down on the coffee table as I got up pulling her hourglass-curved body from the sofa. As we stood in the blur of our cozy surroundings of a blaze fighting higher against the neighboring flame to be the element that it is. I kicked my shoes to the side, along with my shirt and pants as I held both her hands while the silence of her lips listened to my voice.

"Halina, I will not just love every part of you in a surge of my

attraction towards your all! Yet I will place myself in front of your feet of pain, and become the soul narrator of your love story not yet written until all has begun right at this very moment. Let your **Violet and White Wide Leg Cami Jumpsuit** fall from your body down beneath us; allow me to move in closer as my briefs meet the fabric of what has fallen from you. Let me remove the smooth **Strapless Bra** from your skin, departing it from the heart that needs to last... but if you can make your wheel power drive a bit further. Allow me to slide your **Seamless G-String** from your *Yoni* to soon feel my unbroken promise, fulfilling this new covenant of romance you have summoned. As we stand naked in the heart of this horseshoe of fire within this fine room, let all the negative shit be removed as I handle you with my deepest love against the fatality that I will not let have you. Hold the nakedness of my body... tenaciously, and let us become a charm as the smoke of our cigars becomes the conduit to a higher realm of healing."

We were like two important recipes placed in life's preeminent feast and into the oven as we rise with the heat of the room; a glitch of time is lost while lying flat upon this **Cigar Brown Leather Curved Sofa.** Our kiss becomes closer and wild like the cigar smoke settling over the **Marble Ashtray**.

Our bodies then rose, separating our dancing mouths as *Halina* gave me this look with eyes filled with the fear of not existing. To keep my premise, I wrapped the softness of her left hand tight around the extension of my warm mainline. *Halina* closed her eyes, squeezing the tears at her corners as she pulled me inside of her *Yoni* with her right hand firmly at her right breast. She spoke to me with a calm voice!

"Mmmm... Levi, please place your warm suck of lip, and tongue upon my nipples while I take your long walk into my bliss as I flood the shaft of your phallus."

As I looked down at *Halina* below me, she was in full seduction with gentle movements of true unquestionable passion which I had not experienced in a while. This felt genuine, almost like I'd been in love with this woman for ages. I stopped thinking so deeply, and I came down to her right nipple and gave her that work as I pushed my meat deep into her *Yoni* with my right hand gripping the shake of her thick back loving. My hands were rubbing, my hips were shifting, and my mouth was full of her bosom; I was trying my hardest to take her mind off everything except us. I glanced to my side and saw that our cigars were dyeing down which was not an option within the moment we were in. So, I released her breast from my mouth, and with my left hand I grabbed our cigars and hit them both to give them air; I gently placed *Halina's* cigar at her lips. We puffed and pumped and sweat and thrust until we reached a moment of sensation without thought. The moment I stopped to feel my release; *Halina's* right foot kicked me back out of her and fell back onto the sofa puffing my cigar confused. *Halina* then sat up on the sofa with a satisfied yet incomplete look on her face as she spoke softly but briefly.

"Levi, I hate the feeling of something inside of me that I don't understand just taking me out before I am able to do so much more; I hate that this heart disease is determining my fate no matter what I do. I'm a strong melanin woman but sometimes I get so damn afraid to not see what I went to sleep seeing… which is this life that I once had! I am a woman that lives life to the fullest nature but this damn disease wants to erase me, Levi. I don't know what else to do!"

"Halina, look, I won't give you some sorry story of hope but I damn sure can give you a part of me. Every day that you feel like a part of you is dying, I will embed more life into you… rather it's a smile or sitting at the beach for hours or making love to you while I catch your tears. What I'm saying is, in my line of business with my family… I caught two bullets close to my heart and thought I was dead for sure but I am here making love to you, and happy I survived. Just know, you will survive this, just trust me, Ok!"

"Okay, Levi!"

"Halina, let us conquer your inner fight tomorrow but not tonight, let me continue to clear your mind once more, and more; lay back for me and let me taste your confidence. Let me learn to love you in every way because I will never let you down. I will love you to life."

58

"I love you Levi... Mmmm... taste me!"

The Poet

B. GKL

Brotha GKL / Gawd Keenny L io'Et

STORY 3:
MRS. SWEET DAME'S NIGHTSPOT

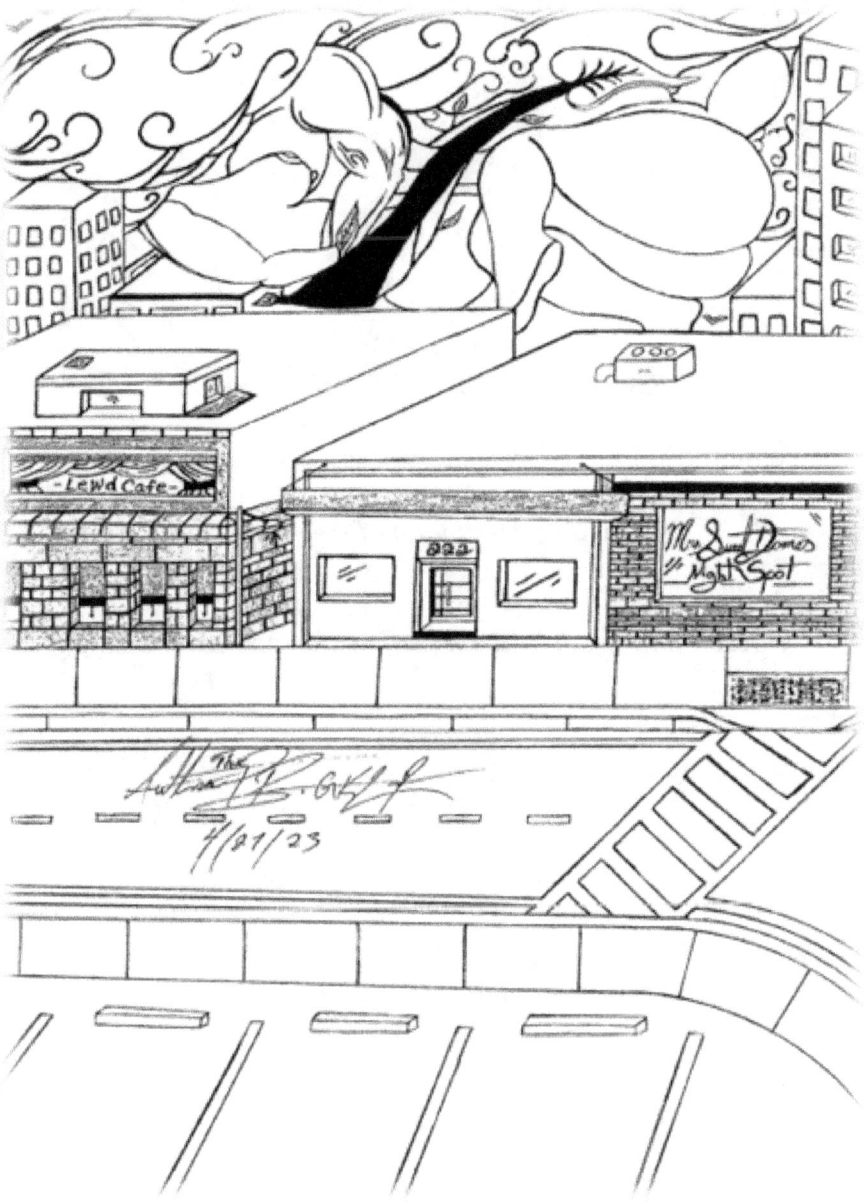

STORY 3:
MRS. SWEET DAME'S NIGHTSPOT

Yoni- *The essence of women's universal life-giver and love.*

Kween- *The truest form of the real queen.*

Characters:
Oberon *[oh - b uh - r aw n]* - *Bearlike,* and **Mrs. Dame**

Before I drove an hour back from my condo towards the inner city to feel that concrete breeze of the midnight hours, I had to handle a well-awaited meeting with two of my most valuable clients from the Deep South. I considered both of them the most unorthodox couple I have seen so deeply in love. I respected their majestic manners, along with their unique bohemian earthy style of clothes and infallible aura of goodwill. They were powerful people that I have learned to respect more than just clients but as good friends and family.

They always made it their business to come from out of town to feel the northern inner-city life and converse wisdom with me, as wife and husband they were made for each other. His wife loved purchasing my edible essential hush-hush oils and they both loved buying all the new rare herbs that I have grown with my divine hands of patience. My clients have high respect for my products and honor the natural healing effects of their pure scent and the qualities of curing all deep inner illnesses. I always enjoyed inviting the married couple to my home for our meetings; to treat them cordially to my place of peace for some wine and to break bread. We all sat while brainstorming at my dinner table on ideas on subjects of true life and universal wisdom. After a couple of hours, the meeting came to an end, and I and my client's parted ways at my driveway with a smooth farewell as their car drove off into the ambiance of the night. I then got into my car and took an hour's drive out into the inner city to feel the hours of midnight; only to clear my mind of all this mental striving.

Driving down the road with all of what was spoken at the meeting with the essence of business running through the fatigue motion of my being as I cruised forward. Traffic was clear and the gas tank needle was comfortably sleeping on "F" on the way out without any other meetings in the books. So, I just continued to rest my one hand on the arch of the leather steering wheel… firmly like. I released the sleep from my body through a calm yawn that walked from the wolf-like stretch of my jaw howling to awaken my mellow muscles as I relaxed my right arm behind the head of my passenger seat.

After an hour's drive down the highway, I decided to take a random exit to see what was new in the streets full of midnight mischief. As I drove down unfamiliar streets while embracing the loud sounds of the nightlife. I then slowed down when I noticed three well-overdressed women walking with two serious-faced brothers who looked more like the lady's security than any type of acquaintance.

My curiosity then motivated me to pull over into a nearby parking lot of a restaurant that was closed for the night. As I set parked, I watched the odd five as they continued to walk; they stepped into this small one-floor diner with gold mirrored windows reflecting the world on the outside of its establishment. Unable to see beyond the windows, my heart wanted to investigate the perplexity of this place after seeing the next group of six women come out after the five went inside. They all were wearing red leather gloves, and boots, holding red leather briefcases, and two red bags wearing beautifully long silver fur coats upon their shoulders. I no longer was tired by far; as the existent stimulation in my driver seat positioned my leg to straighten out after seeing the flavor of six ladies that just flocked to their luxury cars parked across the way. I felt weird because this building seemed too strange and dead-looking to receive or exit out such random mismatched sets of guests.

Since I was in need of something to drink to rid myself of parched words why not just go over to check it all out, I also didn't want to look like a stalker waiting for a snatch of some hens unwilling to roost. So, I decided to get out and leave my vehicle in its place as I headed to my car trunk while paying no mind to rather or not, I was being watched but it damn sure felt like it. I removed my formal business attire and shoes and changed to a linen set and footwear that I kept pressed and ready in the trunk for random occasions like this. I begin rubbing on some of my special scents from my collection, **The Caramel Carbon Oil**. I tapped both of my wrists and onto the lining of my neck and the under collars of my shirt to never leave an oil streak behind; the curiosity began building up in my hands as I continued freshening up my appearance a bit.

As I groomed myself, I decided to take a look around the car trunk and saw a Silverback Rose Royce and a man opening the door for what seemed to be a very important woman. I watched her step out with a demanding force as the gentlemen held her right-hand fingertips as she got out. Then she placed her left hand around his underarm upon his bicep to feel his inner kingdom and the wild nature of his monolithic build. He stood still like a soldier at ease with an emotionalist face, his facial expression cold as a statue in the winter of Detroit.

This *Madam* then uses the signals of her eyes towards the man to do something as she stands, and then he randomly kneels to kiss the ankle of her crocodile boot. He then stood back up slowly at ease with a solid face as she rubbed his strong chin with the nail tip of her middle finger. I couldn't take my eyes off of her from the distance I stood; she wore a crocodile skintight body suit that squeezed her loveliness as if the croc was still alive gripping the life from her; along with small cuts of dark skin shown through her outfit as she stands whispering to the tall gentlemen in a gray suit. Her war locs were set against her thighs and all around as she walked forward with a brass cane with the head of a diamond grizzly bear at the crown of this walking stick as she held it tightly. The beauty of her, and the powerful rousing saunter she gave just pulled me in within the gaze of my watch; the tall man then walked ahead of her to open the building door for the *Madam*.

I then closed my trunk while watching the bottom backside of the *Madam's* magnificent peach disappearing from my eyes into what I assumed to be an odd diner. I only assumed it to be a dining place after seeing some kind of full red bags that two of the six women were carrying with them to their luxury cars earlier. Then I saw the tall man walk out of the diner to the Silverback Rose Royce and drive off; seeing all this appeased my wonder of having some involvement in what this might be. I locked my car as I quickly jogged across the street to the front door with hopes of meeting the *Madam* in the skintight crocodile suit on the inside.

But before I could grab the door handle, a light-skinned Amazon woman exited the place wearing long silk and a very transparent dress. She smiled at me softly with the brightest smile I have ever encountered. As she walked past me, she gracefully touched the top vein of my left hand with hers while walking past my loitering body stuck in my position at the outside of the door. This woman left me with the sight of her see-through dress from the front to her back, gifting me with a view of her triple-pierced *Yoni* as her purpose naturally fills the ambiance with her vast feminine energy flowing around me. She then jiggled softly with her stacked and toothsome existence towards her motorcycle of power.

I watched every motion with a smirk, and I grew curious to see how she would ride out on her chopper with her full candy seen by all the night stars in the midnight. She looked over at me as she erotically lifted her see-through silk dress a little while throwing the chopsticks from her hair onto the ground, and she smiled sliding the key into her ignition. Starting the chopper without any use of a helmet, her chopper growled down the street like a wild animal ravenous for concrete. This woman left my mind shattered from my left hand down to the heart of my phallus; I was more than deeply motivated to walk further ahead without any more second-guessing or wondering what the hell was going on in this place.

Walking in, I expected to be mentally thrown by what I might see in this place when I walked in. With all that I saw coming in here along with the well-flavored eye candy of the Amazon woman I had just seen ride off on her motorcycle… I had to come in. But I found myself standing in my own shadow inside an old diner with vacant tables and seats with no one sitting at the bar. But there stood one bartender, a very gorgeous older Madam in her late 50s behind the bar cleaning wine glasses while humming. She then spoke gently but yet not to greet me but to inquire about my intentions, as she began to ask me one question with her back turned while continuing with her task of tending to her work. I watched her plump blueberry lipstick speak from the reflection of her face in the large mirror behind the liquor as she spoke to me calmly.

"Are you here to dine in, or do you have an appetite for the most superior meals of your tasteful life, my delectable mister?"

I gazed at her mirror reflection confused but intrigued by the riddling question. I thought to myself **"It would be rude of me to be asked a question in someone's place of business without answering back".** So, I took a chance and used my quick wit and silver tongue to give whatever consequence received after my words were spoken. I then answered this provocative classy Madam.

"Whatever is on your menu that is filling, but I would rather be the urge for what you feel should be considered for my craving. I would hate to be left in the desire of being famished… so what would you recommend for me my aromatic sweetness."

The **Kween** smiled as she stopped cleaning the wine glasses and turned around to me, and began reading my body language as she looked me up and down to figure me out. The bartender then moistened the inner shape of her hearted plump blueberry-glossed lips as she spoke to me.

"Well then… we welcome you to Mrs. Sweet Dame's Nightspot, and please savor the best meals we have on our agenda tonight. Nothing is ever for sale but offered by permission upon the preference of what your taste may be."

I smiled at the bartender as I stood in the middle of the diner floor in a deep wonder. The woman stepped to her left and grabbed a gold dart under the bar and threw it past my face to a target on the wall and the entire middle floor under me began descending underground. I firmly stood in my space as I descended into the diner's floor. I looked up watching the diner's ceiling become smaller while going at least a mile down as everything closed above me. The floor stopped suddenly, placing me in the sight of a large hallway covered in cherry woodgrain everywhere. I was hesitant to move, as I gazed at the most glamorous unclothed paintings against the walls, and the statues positioned in unique ways alongside the wide range of polished walls. The solid art has shown me the forthcoming consummation through solid stones of love stories. I would have never imagined seeing such visual masterpieces in the depth of such a place like this.

I then decided to step forward off the platform that anchored me down here to this incomprehensible level of intimate repose. Continuing to walk slowly towards what seemed to be a dead end down further. Then the wall at the end begins to elevate revealing a charcoal-colored steel door; the door reminded me of an enormous vintage bank vault. Looking around but walking ahead further as the platform that sent me down here began to rise back up to the diner; I was left with no way of turning around to leave at any time.

I then made it to the vault but before I could even fathom turning away my steel of inner will wanted me to enter… pushing me forward. Parts of the wall on each side of me begin to open in the shape of two regular doors hidden from plain sight. 2 palatable women then came out from both sides, coming from the right and the left of me with no expressions other than to conduct important business. Both women stood at "5'1" with real tribal war uniforms fitting snugly to the body. Both of their outer zippers were missing but expressing the free spirit of the **Yoni** being out and squeezed; their war uniforms compressed to their bodies of hoarded wealth against the gems of their soft skin.

They both stood on the sides completely silent with long curly course hair down to the honeyed grace of their bosoms. I watched them talk to one another with their eyes and give orders as to what duties to perform on me as an unknown guest of a new arrival. I was standing there silent and distracted by the mystical approach of both women standing near me profiling me with their eyes. They both took hold of one of my arms and raised my hands outward pulling my wrist towards each side of the wall. They locked both of my wrists to brass chains with cuffs pulled from the wall's hidden places. I started to stop them at the beginning until I noticed the Battle Axes they carried on their waistlines on leather holsters. So, I figured it was best for me not to underestimate the situation and just play along since I decided to come this far. After hearing the locks on my wrist, they both kneeled to my ankles and repeated the same locking ritual… brass cuffs and chains.

I thought to myself, **"I won't lie, I defiantly was worried at this point but hoping this all makes sense soon but I don't believe in regrets and I took the chance to come into this damn place."** They then stood up from my ankles, and the one on the left stepped back into the corner by the vault and pulled another chain located behind the hidden wall. As she pulled the chain my shackles got tighter, and then I roared out in discomfort and yelled out to them… **"This has gone too damn far for me and I wanted to leave!"**

But the woman on my right quickly hand taps the flogger whip on her right hip with anger on her face; she then used her Battle Axe to cut my linen shirt from my body. All I could do was watch a part of my clothes fall to the floor. The woman on the left side then decided to use hers instead, and address my bare chest with her flogger whip; I was struck across my heart but not for suffering but more of a small amount of pleasurable pain. She looked me in my eyes as if to say don't make her have to use severe hostility.

I then looked forward while losing my inner patience as the woman on the left came close to me. She tied a leather belt around my head covering my mouth as she proceeded to the next steps. I stood there in chains while silenced by the elegance of 2 beautifully aggressive nectarous women. I believed that they were performing what I assumed to be a ceremony for all new arrivals before they allowed entry into the vault door. The woman on the left continued securing me as the one on my right stood guard with her arms crossed; my eyes couldn't stop looking at the vacant zippers of both women as their *Yoni's* became swollen gaps of authority.

The woman on the right walks up to me grinning as she then completely strips the rest of my attire from my body in seconds; my shoes, pants, and briefs are thrown to the side hitting the floor as my soul and body remain firmly overt in this large hall of art. I was now unable to speak or have any motion; the woman on my right continued her examination after my clothes were freed from my person. She then randomly pricked my thigh to test my blood for anything harmful that may affect what hides behind this vault of curiosity. The woman on my right then walked over to the other dame to test my blood, and then they both nodded their heads in a positive manner. I already knew that they would find my entire body in perfect form for me to proceed beyond whatever this all might be. I assumed after all of what I just experienced that we were done, and I could be released to go further; instead, they had 2 more steps for me to take before I could go forward.

Both women begin placing their weapons on 2 brass hooks on the wall along with their snug tribal war uniforms; the woman on my left pressed a button near the vault. A vast square in the ceiling above my head opens up slowly with a grand showerhead made of large gemstones of jade pointing down at me. A soft sponge and body wash come down on a shower rack from another hidden compartment in the cherry wood ceiling from above. I looked down when I heard another smaller hole reveal itself in the floor between my feet exposing a brass drain. I looked back up at the women while getting pissed by all the uncanny scrutiny and games. But then the perfect temperature of lukewarm almond milk with small hints of honey rained down on me.

I then accepted this spiritual shower of liquids mastering every part of my flesh as I looked upward feeling the lavation fall over my bound physical structure. I allowed this cleanse to fall upon my kinky nappy chest and far down to my waistline. I watched the umpteen trickles of almond milk, and a hint of honey drizzling through my curly-coated black yard; while surrounding the implement of what I have as my greatest tool to landscape any flatlands of Butterfly Pea flowers in need of ambitious labor.

So, with my eyes now closed upward to the purifying dribbles with my soul's face and body cleansed by the pour down. I then was unaware of when the women would cease with this in-depth shower I was under. But then I felt the warmth of both women getting closer against my skin, followed by syrup-like drizzles of fresh coconut body wash coating my wholeness as the soft sponge was lathered around me, under and over. My eyes remained closed and I heard the sponge fall towards the puddle beneath me with the bottle of coconut body wash hitting the wet floor. The shower ran over me as it then switched to warm water; the two women washed the soapy foam from my face as I opened my eyes to see them both stand before me. So, at this point I already speculated the last step that was coming from this process using my keen intuition, I believe that they would now let me enter the vault doors.

But then the woman on the left pulls 2 chains from behind the wall, and the water shuts off. The drain hatch closed, and the shower head and rack became hidden once more. She then pressed a button in the wall to activate the room warmers to begin the drying process. The woman on the right then came close to me to remove the leather belt from my mouth and head and placed it behind the door she came out of. She then leaned in towards me to take one long chocolate ice cream lick across my collarbone as she navigated her left hand down the right side of my inner thigh. She used her right hand to lay it flat against my pre-wet abdomen as the woman on the left looked at me as if she wanted war; she stood there holding a cold look that would devour any man's energy.

So, I started looking towards the left and right of me. I stood in this hallway staring at this large vault door, and I gazed at the two divinely naked women with over-serious faces as they gazed hard at me. I then assumed to myself that these irresistible women are the guardians of this damn vault door and I believe that they get to decide rather it opens or not. But through all of my deep thinking while standing here unclothed, chained, and cuffed in the middle of this hall. I was at least relieved that my mouth was no longer covered to speak my mind. But then I did notice one very important fact about both women, they never talked, not even once but they inner stood their task; this was all too different for me because it made it hard for me to read their intentions without hearing the tone of their personalities.

Before my thoughts could dive any deeper, I felt the room suddenly becoming dry once more. I watched the woman on the left of me walk behind me with a lustfully corrupt smile, and then I was damn sure worried at this point; only because the chains were viselike with every part of my flesh revealed to a hallway of hidden luxuries. But while in thought, the other woman on my right stood beneath my furlike chest just grinning. Her eyes had plans, so I knew now this was my time to speak before things went against my strict mental list of bizarre erotics that I was willing to indulge in.

But before any of my words could gather a retort. I was then choked into a brutish grunt as the naked woman that stood behind me lassoed sheer fresh panties tight around my throat. As she pulled my neck my head and back went backward into an umber arch of pain with her small but strong knee pressed forward in my lower spine. My chest protruded as the chains got tighter upon my wrists and ankles as I stood arching backward. The woman in front of me continued to watch my eyes as they became bitter red vines and my breathing was left with little air to obtain. The soft dangling fabric and sheer fresh pantie line across my throat only allowed me to grunt and jerk in anger. The "5,1" woman in front of me became more strange with ambition as she securely seized the girth of my genius and stroked my knowledge to its full length to test the magnitude of my durable wisdom.

I honored the way that she suctioned my four cinnamon ice scoops, and downward to the base of my cone upon my wooly cotton candy and apricots in a flawless duet of suspension. She could give a brain freeze to a polar bear eating a shivering arctic meal in a freezing dive. At this point, the bondage of my airway was no concern after I felt the swell of her tonsils; her upper and lower lips dragged my merciless ship to the dock of her soft palate secreting a drenching warmness. The woman behind me then removed her knee from my spine and released the sheer fresh panties from my throat as my soul's bones began to samba dance within my skin. The woman in front of me continued to exert my glans tip to the root, with her gentle palm in possession of my pillowcase full of viscid dreams on the Milky Way. The woman behind me placed her right leg over my right shoulder with the words *"French Kiss Me Slowly-like"* tattooed around the ankle bone of such a beautiful foot to motivate a new refined fetish.

Her left leg positioned a centered balance with the floor as her hands began seizing my external oblique. I could only value the clinched Freesia flower blossom aroma of her *Yoni* tightly yawning; a smiling yawn as she holds a pose of standing splits behind me as her rotating ankle awaits my mustached furtherance of lips upon her. I then decided once more to just enjoy what is curiously misunderstood with the words **"WHY NOT"** creeping through my loins. My body starts to give way to the woman in front of me testing my staying power as the chains held me in place. The sensation of blissfulness begins to rule my lower front line. So, I faced my intimate hazing. I then leaned my neck over to French kiss the ankle bone of the woman behind me as her right foot dangled over the right muscle of my shoulder. My lips became sultry with smooches against her anatomy and against the blood vessels running through her leg to her illustrious foot.

Before I was cast deeper into this quaint trio of cryptic consummation as I was reaching my crest of ascending tides with the twosome participants, a brass horn came out from the ceiling. The twosome women saw the brass horn and stood at ease without hesitation. They stopped all motility and stood pleasurably naked against both sides of the warm walls with their heads looking down towards the floor. Then a syrupy mellow voice of a distinguished madam spoke rigorously to the two guardian women that placed me in shackles of divine impulse.

"My revered charmers of my establishment, I believe you have tested our new visitant well enough my lovable protectors. Release him, and clothe him in our finest short silk kimono boxers and a robe. Let our vault be open to our new member, and to you benevolent sir, you are now a member rather you concur or not.

Also, secrecy is taken very gravely at the level you have reached, so, be cautious with your life my wonderful tycoon. Welcome to Mrs. Sweet Dame's Nightspot, and know that I am always watching. So, misbehave in the ways that we love and not like a miscreant but a humble crowned head with a need to observe the mystique of a sweet howling debauchery."

After the **Madam** spoke the brass horn retracted back into the ceiling and the two women promptly stepped back behind the hidden openings of the left and right wall. The woman on my left stood in place as the other woman on my right stepped forward holding a warm steamed towel; the scent of its wet warmness was mint and harvest wheat. She gently dabbed me to keep my tool clean of all cruel pleasance. After she purged me of her lusty secretions of suction from my lever with a lukewarm fondle of completion. She then stepped back towards the right at ease just as the other woman continued in place, and both ladies stood firmly without any emotions upon their souls of facial marvelousness. Then they both clothed themselves with *"Gold Laced See-Through Mini Robes"* as they looked up in unison over at me. They lifted their right and left arm behind the wall and the chains released from my limbs.

My arms dropped to my sides and I placed my feet a bit closer to securely maintain my footing as I looked at both sides towards the two women. I felt like a vintage nude painting waiting for a verbal depiction of my meaning at a museum. But for some reason, I was not as angry as I thought I would be once they released me, yet I am enchanted by both women and the unpredictability of being at *Mrs. Sweet Dame's Nightspot*. While analyzing things in my mind, the woman on my left walked forward with a set of perfectly folded short silk kimono boxers and a robe in hand for me to wear. She stood in front of me looking through my energy with such perception and clairvoyance. I then spoke calmly to the short sweetness as she pulled my sight into hers.

"Allow me to take these clothes off your hands so that I may continue forward, I appreciate you *Kween* but I can dress myself beloved. No discourtesy intended towards *Mrs. Sweet Dame's Nightspot* and her rules but I can take it from here if that's ok with you."

The woman took her eyes off me and looked back at the other woman on my right to receive her input on my request to clothe myself. The woman on my right nodded her head in agreement as the sweetness in front of me turned back to me and handed me my clothing. She then stood back at ease at her position on the left. I placed the robe around me with my arms sliding through the sleeves along with the boxers going under my feet to my waistline. I took a deep breath that came from my abs inner impatience followed by a look on my face of **"WHAT NOW."** The two women stepped back further into each movable barrier while the walls closed in front of them. They left me in view of an unopened vault door, waiting alone but not unsure of this occasion concealment I have come upon.

Suddenly, the bellowing of gear chatter with metal turning and grinding like a vast vintage clock of times deception; the vault opened gradually showing its sealed luminousness of trapped candlelight escaping its opening door trim. Abrupt sounds of live Reggae Jazz and all of its background melodic instruments shouted through my ears and pounded through my heart. My pulse thumped enormously with every hit of all steel drums; inner standing the skin-hardening flicks of all kinds of guitars being stroked with emotional strum. As rum poured slowly onto bosoms, down the rib cages, and onto the wilderness, the blow of many horns and trumpets continued wind worshipping the element of air. The collision of music and my soul is now clutching the strike of the congas slapping against the palms, the touch of all piano keys caressing the relieved scales while the cowbells cracked like thunderous clacks of hollow steel. The large room was just hypnotized by the rattlesnake shake of the tambourine releasing its chanted venom into all standing near its quivering rounded fangs.

My eyes then swallowed the sight of steep Marble Onyx stairs leading down to great depths of immaculate social varieties. I had never seen a steamy heated pool crafted for miles along underground with high arched curved ceilings of stone reaching over all that I could see. I had never seen a galore of people from all walks of life just frolicking without any worries; free from cruelty and judgment by those who can't overstand having an imagination for a pleasure ground for adults to leave their realities, and live their royal passions. Now that the vault door is completely open, I stride forward onto the Marble Onyx landing above the towering steps looking down at all the unconcerned strangers fulfilling their lewd appetites. But as I stood looking downward, the vault door behind me began closing. I glanced behind me watching the well-lit hallway become lightless as the vault closed tight with pressure. I turned back to the steps in front of me and I noticed a brass plate on the wall with an engraving that states.

"Descend from the plane of 56 steps and plummet down into the ideas of new, and take a chance of positive stimulus and become vitality as you walk centered within the gold lines."

After reading the brass engraved plate, I noticed that there were no handrails to secure my walk down into this new frequency. There was only the sight of wide treads of Marble Onyx steps, and two gold lines to walk between for all that chose to travel the path without falling from the sides or stumbling down its depth. I descended, walking centered down 56 steps with only moments in between myself and a full pit of libidos driven to drive. I felt unseen as I came down the Marble Onyx steps but when I reached the fifty-sixth step onto the main floor, I was then approached by what I assumed was a receptionist. This woman made the past vintage styles of classy attire missed in the present time as we stood. Her pompadour was superb, her Emerald Techno Swing dress fit her every elegant curve as her ankles complimented her peep toe stiletto heels, she sauntered in with such a guiltless smile.

As she walked toward me with excitement pressed in the rich bones of her cheeks smiling with love to give. I remained firm with my vision occupied with all that I did not expect surrounding me, the receptionist stood blurred within my peripheral. The perky receptionist just waited near me expressing her impeccable dimples with braces placed across her beautiful teeth. I admired the fire from the brick wall candles glaring upon her glazed heart-shaped lips. She patiently waited for me to soak up my entire ambiance before she gave me guidance. I felt the cheers of voices in a moaning bliss. There was a howling of live Reggae Jazz blowing past my silk kimono boxers and around my robe like an open window with sheer drapes barely hiding the frame of my brawny build.

I could see the Live Reggae Jazz band far beyond the pool that stretched in miles of heated water. Undried bodies relaxed in the mood to be wooed by all that stood in exotic clothing or partially nude. I didn't see the great madam of this place, nor did I see the two tribal women who held me in chains within a hall of uncertain plans. The receptionist continued to hold back with patience; she waited as I admired the large crest of a grizzly bear engraved into the stone walls from all sides down towards the end. I saw so many women for me to engage with… plus size, curvy, fit, and slender with many more to appreciate. I then took hold of my focus and looked over at the perky receptionist as she broke her silence and began to speak calmly to me.

"Grand Awakening sir, I am the superior receptionist here and my name is Iguana, and welcome to the main floor of Mrs. Sweet Dame's Nightspot. Let me quickly brief you on some things. The Madam of the house is not a Mrs. because of traditional marriage purposes. The Madam is yet more of a woman committed to the genuine union between the pleasures of the human body and one's higher self. She wheels the power to soulfully elevate the pureness in the divine feminine and divine masculine energies.

Also, understand this; Mrs. Sweet Dame's Nightspot is not some cathouse for aroused rabid women or men to empty their horny burdens. This is a safe oasis for old-fashioned adult amusement to reverse frustration or any hindrance; a home to enjoy life's forgotten joys within the light of those in need of not being judged by the prude world that lies to themselves every day. Humanity is full of walking contradictions that are too afraid to just take the prude flavors out of their heart and caress life with class. So, respect everything that you see here with an open mind, and please do not upset Mrs. Dame or her place or the outcome will be critical on your behalf. What name would you like us to address you as majestic one?"

I grinned while ignoring her kind threats because again, I inner stood all the precautions after all of what I had seen so far with such exuberant hospitality. So, I answered the nocturnal beauty with love in my voice.

"Well *Iguana*, just call me Oberon, and for the record, I just don't overstand how could anyone treat this place badly at all. Mrs. Dame has nothing to worry about when it comes to me and making trouble. But I do have high hopes to meet Mrs. Dame upon my soul front within this place of touch and feel!"

Iguana looked at me with her right hand positioned on her right curvy

76

hip and had her left hand angled up toward the ceiling in salute above the brow. She placed her feet in a firm twist against the ground with the vibes of a gentlewoman of true high rank of a sorority style formed to perfection.

Iguana's pose silently signaled a petite woman with a skin tone of nutmeg with cinnamon-colored hair in a Pineapple Updo. This woman walked towards me with a pencil, notepad, a waiter's silk vest, and her name tag that read *Lucent*. She was barefooted with her trimmed *Yoni* uncovered in the open grasping the warmth of this vast room as she swayed towards me upon *Iguana's* signaled request. I thought to myself that this place could send anyone without an open mind to an early tomb of pleasure just from the sights in one's own eyes. Luckily, I am not a disagreeable person and am very venturous.

Lucent then came towards me as she looked beyond my presence with her eyes locked on *Iguana; Lucent* stood humbly while waiting on *Iguana's* dictation. I just stood and gazed at this petite woman sent to me with such a mind-dripping bareness of pleasantness. *Iguana's* voice then cut through the pleasant but thunderous sounds around us as she spoke to *Lucent* softly but sternly.

"Lucent, this gentleman here is Oberon, and I want you to make the Grand Madam's establishment a home for him as we do for all of our guests. Oberon, Lucent will be your private temporary waitress and guide for today... just until you get the hang of things around here. Maybe I will personally tend to you later but only if you are worthy beyond your tour and have earned your way. Also, treat Lucent with respect and allow her to approve or disapprove of any desires you may have towards her, Oberon please enjoy yourself!"

I watched *Iguana* nod her head to *Lucent* as she sauntered away into the crowd of women and men feeding off this incredible energy that addictively filled the air. *Lucent* then spoke to me in excitement to get things started. I over stand that if anyone I knew had this opportunity, they would have definitely jumped body and mind first into all that I see in my eyes. But one thing about me is that I am a man with a patient hunger, one who is drawn to incomprehensible women with much to research and value.

Lucent then broke my deep thinking by asking me to follow her. As she stepped in front of me swaying in her divine feminine as she walked with a switch in her waist. Her bare feet left imprints of heat in the form of her barefooted walk against the smooth floor. The hot print of her feet faded as she lifted her foot arch and warm toes from the surface of the Marble Onyx floors. Random naked bodies danced across our forward path in a comfortable stagger as they walked from the long glass bar against the stone wall into the pool of all kinds of copulation. I watched people move out of *Lucent's* way as we strolled through the crowd like two luxury cars cruising through the night strip casing the scene.

Lucent's petite body lured me behind her jiggling tight ripples which became wavelike across her tail end as the heel of her bare feet pressed against the Marble Onyx flooring. Then the swollen print of my boxers started to gain weight as my warm blood vessel beat against my inner thigh as I walked behind *Lucent.* The luminous party lights ahead of us passed in between the gapped walk of her trimmed *Yoni* as she guided me on her tour. The live Reggae Jazz continued to flow around us as every guest gratified their needs with the countless chests that felt the friction of palpitating breasts. The sound of a murmuring tongue requesting to have silver candle wax poured upon the belly. I watched the sight of warm slow wax pouring upon the gut of a beautiful plus-size woman; the melt ran down her silky side rolls. This beddable woman spiraled her afro *Yoni* up and down a gentleman's deeply inserted key; the silver wax dripped from him into the pool of nookie.

I have never seen so much leather, toys, and contraptions utilized just to elate the body to unworldly sexual limits of sensations undetermined. The live music pursued its pour of cadence through us all. Flowering plants of orchids were released from the hands of a coupled woman and man in silk garbs. They set upon wide swings that hung from the high arched curved ceilings of stone. Orchids fluttered as they fell into the sweltering heated pool of merging souls; as they fell peacefully, channeling something far greater than just a mere climax but a soaring blissfulness and euphoria.

Seeing all this seemed inconceivable by judging the location of this building and the neighborhood it's in, but it's worth discovering after it was revealed in such a sensationally fierce manner. Before my thoughts could go any deeper into any new misdirection's pulling at my focus. I suddenly felt a nice silk fabric caressed over my battered knuckles and the back of my right hand, and the fulfillment of heat in my loose grip. It was the sudden warmness of *Lucent's* velvety bosom compressed in my right hand under her vest as she spoke to me while laughing.

"Oberon, I know that this is a new beginning of your voyage. So, navigate your shaft to reach the distant travel towards the natural waters, propelled by the panting wind of the diaphragm out the Yoni pulling you forward as you stargaze true infinity. But Oberon, you must relax and not look so bewildered when there is much more to indulge. In which you have already had a taste of grand indulgence doing your inspection; you had a taste of our two deadly yet overprotective vault guardians. They held you in chains on the mid-floor entry in our woodgrain hall of alluring art... remember! Let's just continue our walk over to the glass bar to get you a drink but of my choosing since you are new here after all... if you don't mind the risk of my option of what spirits to swig!"

I then looked at *Lucent* and grinned because I admired her poetic way with words as well as her randomness. I am unable to deny her request with such a gift of gab and the eloquence in her voice of reason. *Lucent* then removed my right hand from beneath her vest while holding my fingertips ever so lightly in her soft right hand. I followed behind her pace while advancing towards the glass bar that was shelved with countless amounts of exotic liquor that only one could imagine sipping. There were so many names of bottled spirits that I could not pronounce or have seen anywhere else.

This glass bar ran along the full length of the stone wall down to the end of it all. I decided to just take a seat at the bar on a glass bar stool with gold LED lights glowing within it as *Lucent* stood to my left with her pencil, and pad wearing only her silk vest. There was so much going on around me that I couldn't keep up with the motion of the ambiance filled with all to relish as I looked at *Lucent's* enchanting side view as she signaled a barmaid a way down. I couldn't see the barmaid clearly as she walked toward us because of all the party lights flaring in my eyes.

The barmaid came forth into clear sight; she was a ripped woman with the perfect balance of a salacious muscular vixen coming from a war to stand as a gladiator *Kween*. This striking woman had savage mercenary written within her eyes; along with entrancing etched into her beautifully robust half-naked physique of divine femininity. She stood about "5'6"… curvaceous, and dainty and she was a vigorous bodybuilder with the skin tone of sandalwood.

This barmaid wore the gold head of a howling wolf centered upon her sternum attached to a gold necklace that linked to her pierced breast. The necklace connected from her nipples down to her navel underneath her gold chainmail armor skirt that made noise when she sauntered the floor. The barmaid had curly course hair twisted in two very long ponytails hanging down her gluteal fold of perfection. All and all this woman looked very familiar to me but I just couldn't figure it out until *Lucent* noticed my facial expression towards the barmaid. *Lucent* then decided to explain to me what she assumed my face was trying to figure out as I looked away from the barmaid and toward *Lucent* in confusion.

"Oberon let me introduce you to our top mixologist Meeka, who is also the head of security. Meeka is also the older sister of the two women you encountered outside the vault door in the hall of art."

I then looked back at *Meeka* as her eyes pierced through me with that same cold-ass look that her sisters gave me while doing my body inspection. But *Meeka's* stare was much more brutal than her younger sisters but I could see the family resemblance as I coldly gazed back at *Meeka*. *Lucent* then gave me a quick pinch on the derriere to get me to snap out of the odd staring contest with *Meeka* as *Meeka* stood her ground with her remarkable enduring scent of raw honey and butterscotch. *Meeka* looked fit enough to destroy a coconut with her formidable thighs and her fit structure of bitter, and malignant sweetness. But I stopped myself from thinking any harder and decided to just stick my right hand out to greet *Meeka*. Regardless of how odd the moment felt to me knowing that she knew about the trio I had with her sisters without me having any control over what was going to go down after I stepped out into that hallway.

As my right hand remained extended out to shake *Meeka's* hand to lighten the mood, something quickly felt unpleasant at that point. The moment felt more peculiar when *Lucent* stepped back from the bar with a foxy smile and her arms crossed. I also noticed that *Meeka* didn't blink once after my hand reached out to greet her; that was strange! I blinked for one damn second while thinking too much, and that's when *Meeka* let out a sort of snarling moan. She strenuously leaned over the glass bar like a wild carnivorous huntress with acute eyesight and the speed of something unknown to me. This mind-boggling well-built woman lifted me with incredible speed and strength and placed my body down on the glass bar as if my muscles accounted for nothing. *Meeka* snatched the robe from my body, and stretched me out on top of the glass bar, and lassoed me down to the bar top like livestock with rope. I was so damn tired of being restrained in this place of desire and continuously treated like meat to be tenderized by superb women with bizarre ways of flirting.

While all of this shit is happening to me the full room of erotic bodies continued gyrating in elation. They all seemed to overlook my scene without any reaction, other than *Lucent* standing aside watching *Meeka* hold me down while roped to the glass bar. This was the strawberry on top of the cake for me, and I was pissed, I gazed at *Meeka* as she held me down without struggling to hold me flat on my backside. Before I even looked like I was going to cuss, *Meeka* grabbed a bottle of whisky and poured a shot across my lips, and slurped its bitterness from my mouth and neck as she spoke at me with domination in what she was about to convey.

"Oberon or whatever the fuck you wish to be called, I don't give a damn about your handshake or the pleasures you might seek here. I am related to the Madam Dame, and I don't have to respect shit that you are about other than you ordering a stiff drink or me forcing you to fill my glass with your chattering screams while I ride your soul's love muscle into fucking limbo. You are nothing to me but meat that needs to be sucked from the bone, and thrown to thirsty women looking for scraps of an exhausted man to rebuild after my touch upon you. I am Meeka, and what my sisters have done to you upstairs is nothing compared to how I will have your face enslaved between my open gates until you squeal to perish with a dripping chin of sustenance from my bushed tigress. You will smile the entire time kneeling beneath me, unable to speak words but left with only

81

muffled shrieks like a rabbit wishing to get its carrot into the burrow of my earth to nibble softly in the darkness."

I looked at *Meeka* as she spoke to me like a peon or enemy, I didn't over stand *Meeka's* reason or why the belligerence but I knew that I was pissed beyond nature. *Meeka* just stood over me grinning with her hands holding me down to the glass bar in my boxers restrained. I just laid flat and leered at *Meeka's* gold necklace hanging, and linked from her lubricated pierced bosoms down to her rectus abdominis to her gold chainmail armor skirt hiding the forest hidden with 10-karat gold links. *Lucent* continued to watch *Meeka* hold me down as goosebumps appeared on *Lucent's* appetizingly seminude figure standing with a horny foxlike smile. Moments after, 4 irresistible hellishly leather-dressed women pranced forward slowly by the glass bar on my right peripheral vision. These women were pulling 4 thick copper chains tethered to the neck of a 7-foot dark mud-skinned brother in full leather bondage attire. He was covered in leather completely except for his eyes, forearms, and hands.

His hands and forearms were confined to his sides with rhino skin tethers attached to the leather bondage at his waist, and his eyes cased the place with animalistic movements as if he were on a hunt. Everybody kept referring to the 4 women and the towering brother as *The Sirens of Grandiose. The Sirens and Grandiose* seemed to be a unification of polygamists which seemed to stay grouped the way that people kept referring to them as one name most of the time. But as they walked by the glass bar *Grandiose* came to a halt in mid-stride, standing in front of *Meeka, Lucent,* and I. *The 4 Sirens* quickly looked back at *Grandiose* enraged with him for stopping abruptly.

The Sirens standing ahead of *Grandiose* turned around while holding the 4 thick copper chains in fury. All 4 women then pulled out long-handled leather floggers from their hips and aggressively struck *Grandiose* across his forearms and hands in unison. *Grandiose* looked to the high stone ceilings and embraced the painful pleasure and roared with a deep grunt while saying **"YES…LET MY FLESH INHERIT YOUR WRATH"** in a low tone looking back down at *The Sirens* with exuberance. *The Sirens* turned back around holding the 4 thick copper chains while placing their leather floggers back on their hips but stood still as if they knew *Grandiose* had something more to say.

Our surroundings continued onward ignoring us as *Grandiose* looked at *Meeku* standing dignifiedly behind the glass bar and spoke to her with respect but with powerful certitude.

"Meeka, you look rather deviously mesmerizing tonight my thickset gladiolus flower. I would never be one to stop a wolf from devouring what it wants but I am not a fan of teasing my prey or showing mercy when I am hungry for a competitive woman like yourself. When you are done tormenting your dinner, meet us on the next level down in the *"Cave Room of Contentment"*. The Sirens of Grandiose will see you there and don't forget to bring your labia spreader straps; I was hoping to take a look into multiple universes tonight but mainly yours. So, bring your cosmos to me, and let me journey. I will allow you to handle me the same way you have handled this new gentleman you have pinned to the glass bar here. Bring to me your greatest aggression, face me head-on, and let me lightly gnaw on your stellar brawn of divine femininity, Meeka, my conquering *Kween*.

Also, Hello *Lucent* my dainty love with the throbbing kiwifruit that drips for erotic ferocity, *Lucent,* you are doing a sensational job at *Mrs. Sweet Dame's Nightspot* my partially nude mantrap. Make sure this new bastard inner stands the rules around here, and please don't let *Meeka* break the brother before he finishes his tour on his first night here. *Meeka,* I will see you soon, and to you, sir, enjoy yourself because this place is like no other and you have not seen shit yet my friend... welcome to *Mrs. Sweet Dame's Nightspot.*"

Grandiose then went silent while looking away and putting his attention towards his finger-licking *Sirens. The Sirens of Grandiose* just walked away in silence and headed toward the end into the glaring lights of silhouettes dancing and seducing their flavor of infatuations. As I looked back at *Meeka,* her breasts were perky with nipples jutting as her gold chains sounded off like chimes of heavy metal, and her bosoms became electrified by the approach of *Grandios's* spoken words coming and going. *Meeka* watched *The Sirens of Grandiose* fade into the crowd as she held me down tighter to the glass bar. *Meeka* grinds her tongue beneath the top right side of her teeth like a wolf distracted from its meal catching the scent of deadlier prey nearby. As *Meeka* looked away, I grew enraged and yelled.

"MEEKA, UNTIE ME AND BACK THE HELL UP... AND LUCENT, YOU KNOW THAT THIS IS SOME STRAIGHT-UP BULLSHIT RIGHT HERE!"

Lucent snickered with a quick reply, *"Well Oberon, you can always take me to the XL padded Straddle Bench or the leather sling to state your burdensome issues. Just take a plunge into my solar eternal to receive the celestial squeeze of my kiwifruit until you feel the juice of my benevolent never-ending truth."*

I tried ignoring what *Lucent* quoted but for some damn reason, her words carried sensual weight along with her being a great distraction to a man's erotically deepest compulsions for comfort. But in my quick thought of taking eyes off of *Meeka* for just a moment, *Meeka* then reminded me that one should never forget to pay attention to one's surroundings while in an essential dilemma. *Meeka* waits for nothing as I stared over at *Lucent; Meeka* spins me around on the glass bar into a firm choke hold and took her right hand from behind my neck and into the front slit of my boxers. With my cervical spine pressed against the breast gold of her clutch and her left arm across my throat while bound her tense grip held my satchel of loaded stones. Then a beautifully loud bird whistle was heard from afar over the live band and the moaning guest with loud pleasure. *Meeka* looked to her right taking in an annoyed breath and relaxed her grip upon me. *Meeka* gracefully ran her fingernails up the back of my shaft while growling in my ear full of rage. *Meeka* laughed and snitched one single-course hair from my pelvis as she pulled her right hand from my boxers which made me pissed off even more as I begin cussing her ass out.

"MEEKA, what the fuck is wrong with you? Is this bullshit personal or do you just get off on causing me pain? Don't get this erotic shit fucked up! I allowed most of this to happen but damn, you keep coming at me as if you get aroused causing me fucking agony and frustration! So, when in the hell do we get to what this whole tour shit is about without all of what I am assuming is some initiation freaky shit. I'm a gentleman at the end of the day but I won't take no more of this bullshit from you, release my damn neck chick!"

Meeka looked over at *Lucent* and grinned but then that same beautifully loud bird whistle was heard everywhere once more; then a realistic sound of a grizzly bear roared with a huffed growl. That sound off must be serious because it made *Meeka* release me immediately while removing the restraints and she stepped back against the full wall of liquor. I looked over at *Lucent's* skin covered with soft goosebumps of nervousness, and then I truly know that shit got real after that and that whoever sounded off is not to be taken lightly. I stood back to my feet grabbing my robe from the bar top as I looked around me. *Meeka* then spoke once more before she decided to walk away but her tone and actions were different than before.

"Oberon, we are happy to have you here at Mrs. Sweet Dame's Nightspot...please enjoy the rest of your tour and Lucent, you may continue your walk with our new guest."

Then I watched *Meeka's* divine warrior beauty slowly walk away into the bright lights through the crowd of euphoria; she went in the direction of the growling grizzly bear and the beautiful loud bird whistle. Despite *Meeka* crossing the line with me, for some reason I was concerned for *Meeka,* only because of the way she quickly switched up her intentions and left peacefully after hearing the echo of the grizzly and the melodious whistle. *Lucent* looked over at me into my eyes with her exquisite feet pressing against the Marble Onyx floor as she spoke with tender words of ease through my being.

"Oberon, for a man with so little patience, a vast amount of hidden frustration, and a powerful hard drive, you seem to carry your feelings on your shoulders. Your sledgehammer may be substantially imposing for clobbering through walls but your heart seems to reach the broadness of your shoulders; which seems to hit harder when you give a damn beyond your unselfishness and hubris. What I am saying to you is that Meeka will be just fine, she just has to answer to the ruler of this sanctum for taking things too far with potential members on their first day here. Anyhow, before we reach your true destination, I believe that you and I still have some burdensome issues that you may have with my tour... Oberon."

I looked at *Lucent's* glorious build as she spoke to me. I then took in a deep breath as *Lucent* randomly stretched her left arm in the air to give an odd signal. She put up 3 fingers and then the letter "C" with her index and thumb followed with a balled fist; which was closed tight enough to remove all the air from her palm while putting her arm down to her petite side. Suddenly a bartender behind the glass bar walked up to **Lucent** and placed 3 hard double shots of cognac neat in front of her. **Lucent** looked at me with the allurement of her soulful eyes and into my sight as I then questioned her in a deep tone.

"Lucent, am I that difficult of a man that you need to drink that much liquor before moving forward with this weird tour of temptation."

She answered me while rolling her absorbing eyes with a devious smile and tapping her notepad against her thigh.

"No Oberon, these three drinks are for you my dear, because we are about to head to the wooden bridge leading over to that platform in the middle of the pool. We call that The Cage of Glass. That will be the temporary office so that we can discuss any issues that you may have with me and my choices upon where we have stopped on this tour. So, handsome, drink up! You know what; better yet, just bring all three shots with you."

The bartender who was standing by with no emotion in his face then begins placing the 3 double shots onto a brass tray. He then stepped backward crossing his arms against his lower backbone and walked off to serve others. I kept gazing back at the exit but I was unable to turn away and leave this joint; only because I was too enchanted by **Mrs. Sweet Dame's Nightspot,** and **Lucent's** addictive energy of delight that she cast upon me while in her presence. **Lucent** then turned around and started walking as I whispered under my breath... **"Fuck it, why the hell not."** I grabbed my 3 drinks and began heading towards the small wooden bridge. We passed by an elegant orgy with a carousel of plump clouds of fine-smelling green herbs as they lounged on a large leather bed with solid gold Round Head Upholstery Tacks. They sat near the pool by the small wooden bridge that we were heading to.

There was a strong smell of fresh fruits, pure raw honey, and some *"Ooh-La-La"* in the atmosphere. The long-heated pool was overflowing with lewd movements of refined moments to relish with anxious cravings. I observed that free-spirited intimacy served on epic levels of countless climaxes. On the left side of *Lucent* and I was the pool of heat moving like an ocean of mating sea dwellers clashing against the current to manifest their legacy, thereafter. As I walked behind *Lucent* while carrying the tray of 3 hard double shots of cognac balanced and still. Ahead of us on our right side across from the wooden bridge; a beauteous woman of voluptuousness wore nothing but her Nubian Sheba Brown Lipstick and earth-tone eye shadow. This plus size curvy scrumptiousness set upon a Face Riding Sex chair; the center of the seat was cut out. Her *Yoni* was swollen from the pressure from the thickness of her force-tight seated thighs. Her eyes rolled gracefully to the back of her shutters towards her frontal lobes first eye.

There was a man's head, neck, and wrist locked beneath her, forced to taste her throbbing peach. All tongue no teeth with nothing but an inch of distant reach from the *Kween's* refreshing delicacy. He rests flat beneath the Face Riding Sex chair with his back upon a Chocolate Faux Leather Throw. A slender-built seductress stood over him with her feet placed on both sides of his oblique. The slender sweetness was dressed in a dark purple carnival costume with feathers of indigo, blue, green, yellow, and orange.

She was drizzling red grenadine which turned into a stream of syrup down between her heels upon his shivering flesh. The things I have seen in such a short time of just randomly leaving my abode; just to get into something pleasing, and I found more than what I planned for and what I needed. I felt like I was gazing at everything in slow motion while walking behind *Lucent* to the pool's wooden bridge leading to *The Cage of Glass.* When *Lucent* and I reached the bridge, there was a small mixed group of people discussing wisdom, astrology, and libido consciousness. They set a towering Samoan man with tribal ink across his upper torso, and a tender Samoan woman set beside him with tribal ink down her thighs and up between her legs. Setting across from them was a Dominican woman with La Romana seas within her eyes. Beside her was a very fit Jamaican man with locs like jungle vines to the floor, and near him set a calm Russian woman with warlike mannerisms in her as she set still as stone.

With all that went on, I noticed that the small conversing group was wearing comfortable but unique swimming attire. They all had the head of a grizzly bear, which was embroidered on different parts of the fabric. Seeing all that I had seen, from the bar to the pool's wooden bridge gave me the notion; which was never to perceive this place as a predictable bordello but yet a diverse destination of high-class relief. I then dragged my outer lip under the top row of my teeth and then out; I tend to do that when I am no longer uncomfortable, and ready to play the game.

Lucent then tapped one of her Stiletto Fingernails on the bottom of the brass tray of drinks that I was holding in my right hand; I looked at her as she lightly pulled my left hand by the fingertips. *Lucent* pulled me slowly towards *The Cage of Glass* into the center of the enormous heated pool of pleasurable swimming moans. *Lucent* walked into the heart of this transparent room folding her arms and looking at me… with irresistible writing in her stance.

The Cage of Glass had an XL padded Straddle Bench in the middle glass floor. There was a leather sex swing hanging from the right corner, and a short cedar wood column on its left corner. The view around us displayed most of our surroundings but not all. I gazed around me at the clear view of *Mrs. Sweet Dame's Nightspot,* and there were still so many rooms in this place that I could not see from our position. Then *Lucent* dropped what little clothing she wore as she slid a Lace Masquerade Mask upon her face; she then spoke to me in a way that would surely get my attention.

"Hay, Oberon, drink your 3 shots and bring the beast of your soul to me and express your issues with my tour. I want you to scarf down my energy until shrieks of sweat run from my pores. But hurry Oberon, so that you may choose wisely what you would like to use, within this secure Cage of Glass."

I then looked over at the cedar wood column in the left corner ahead. I walked toward it placing the brass tray down upon its flat top; I began guzzling down all 3 double shots of liquid heat without taking any breaks in between. With my back turned toward the cedar wood column, I turned my head slightly to the right. In my peripheral, I saw *Lucent* elevate a different hand signal. *Lucent's* right palm was high in the air, all five of her fingers were pointing down to her inner hand like an eagle's hunting claw. Suddenly the Live Reggae Jazz switched over into a live sensually sorcerous Neo-Soul melody, and the entire mood of the room became romantically vigorous. I watched a full room of warm bodies raise their glasses above all heads, giving a toast towards the live band; as they relaxed all around, and down to the end of the heated pool where the music stormed with right melodies.

I then turned completely around towards *Lucent* as she stood in the middle of *The Cage of Glass,* flaunting her exotic Lace Masquerade Mask; her eyes and mouth uncovered with her petiteness ready for me to express my issues with her tour. Every light in the high ceilings became a reddish honey color. The lights flickered savagely as *Lucent* set upon the XL padded Straddle Bench waiting for me to approach her with my appetite vibrating from my skin.

The Cage of Glass was seen by all that set near or far from its transparent walls as the alcohol of hazy eyes turned to watch us perform a cinema of a lifetime; they wanted to observe a different moment of a new random night visitor. *Lucent* then laid forward with her body lining the top of the XL padded Straddle Bench. Her limbs were positioned on each side of its extra paddings to hold her bent arms and spreading legs, only to receive my unyielding unwritten complaint. Her waist inclined upwards squeezing back the deliquescent yielding of her *Yoni* playing possum. Lying motionless as if she couldn't be suspended from my tree and pull the leaves from it. Then the music begins to play even more alluring within the scenario as the building of eyes watched our every move. So, I began to walk towards the Straddle Bench towards *Lucent;* removing my robe as I walked, letting it fall to the glass floor. As *Lucent* lay stagnant, watching me free myself from the corner of empty shot glasses as I strolled onto her.

As I got closer to *Lucent,* a woman suddenly walked in dressed in a Turquoise Egyptian Kween Cutout dress; this woman also wore the same type of exotic Lace Masquerade Mask as *Lucent.* But the color of this woman's disguise matched her outfit as it nicely held her body's warmth. This woman smelled delicious as *Lucent's* warm structure; this madam was barefooted and rolling in a waist-high bamboo tray with odd things placed upon it. There was a full-headed gold mask of a grizzly bear and 1 hot branding iron with a grizzly bear's footprint.

The tray had a flat stone with items positioned neatly upon it with a fourth double shot of unknown liquor with gold flakes. I stood there in my boxers confused but willing to travel forward as this mystical carrier stood at the entry waiting for me to come forth. So, I changed my direction towards this madam that was patiently waiting for me. I felt all eyes watching every step that I took towards the entry. As I walked, **Lucent** remained arched upward, and forbearing until I made a move against her needs.

I approached the woman as she stood beside the tray, and I looked into this woman's line of sight; her eyes were like an ancient feline initiating a new process of erotic levels for one to reach. With her right hand reaching down she picked up the hot branding iron with a bear's footprint at its end as she began reciting 9 important words to me.

"You may not ask... just trust in the infinite."

I took in the deepest airs of breath that I could conjure from within with only the assumption of what was about to happen in this watched moment. Then this woman looked deep into me with those eyes, and she gestured for me to kneel; her left hand had fingernails like a purring lioness ready to pounce as her left hand pointed tautly at the floor. My right knee began to kneel to the floor before this omniscient woman; the music became more sultry-like, and the people all around stopped moving and held their drinks higher in the air as my knee touched the glass floor. The nameless woman touched my chin lifting my head gracefully, and angled my visual mind to her feline eyes; then her right hand slowly branded my top left Trapezius muscle. I couldn't believe I was kneeling like this in my boxers feeling a pain that was felt all over my body. This woman was different because I couldn't look away while she held my chin towards her. I did not want to interfere with the process by stepping away from the sizzle of a short burning agony. This woman gazed down through my face, watching me intensively as I cleared my mind to try to handle the hot steel against my flesh.

As my left eye palpitated, all my muscles tightened as my right fist pulled at my boxers on my right thigh that was pressed to the glass floor. The woman withdrew the branding iron from my body and she placed it back down to the flat stone. She reached for the next item which would be a fourth double shot for me, but this drink of gold flakes was strange. She then used half of the double shot to pour some libation on my burning bear's footprint that now forever remains on my body; as I cringed from the pain she poured the rest of the drink down into my mouth. My eyes became red and watered from holding in the anguish of the branding irons induction. The woman placed the glass onto the tray and picked up the full-headed gold mask of a grizzly bear and placed it on my head. Then the entire room of erotic souls applauded and yelled out because of what I had just completed. The woman placed her soft left hand on the side of my face gesturing me to rise; I stood up with a strange feeling to growl with euphoria as eroticism ran through my bloodstream. The woman kissed the nose of the gold grizzly bear mask that was placed upon me; she spoke as she turned away to walk out with her rolling bamboo tray and unnatural eyes.

"Oberon, listen to me! A radiant light that shines is considered nothing without darkness to stand behind its soft shimmering brightness; without the night, the light is just lost in its own beautiful luminous. Lucent awaits your wildest darkness, so tend to her light."

As I watched the woman walk out of **The Cage of Glass** to cross the wooden bridge, I turned around to **Lucent,** staring at her through the open eyes of the gold grizzly bear's mask. The painful singe from the branding had me breathing heavily through the gaps of the bear's golden teeth. An overwhelming feeling of staying power boiled within me; I assumed that the last strange drink was beginning to kick in. Because then I felt ready, as every damn vein on my body bulged and beat through every inch of my physique. The room went wild with standing and sitting ovations as they watched me walk toward **Lucent;** I used my right hand to tear my boxers from my V-cut and commenced forward.

The strenuous pulse in my extensive crown tip could dictate the inner principles of true engagements of pleasure; so, as my stiffness led ahead of me as I walked towards the XL padded Straddle Bench. I stood upon this bench holding my issue in my left hand for **Lucent** to sustain. The burning sensation from the bear's foot branded on my left shoulder started to burn; then I began to sweat from the hot lights flashing through **The Cage of Glass.** So, I looked at **Lucent's** inclined arch and began sliding my fingerprints under and front to the back of her trimmed *Yoni*. I rubbed the waters of her compact space upon my branded seared skin. Then *Lucent* whispered to me.

"Ahh Yes, mmm, give me all your concerns and let me feel your thoughts."

Once *Lucent* uttered those words, that same enraged growling of a grizzly bear was heard even louder from the far end of this enormous heated pool. Then my body felt an extreme broiling sensation from that fourth unknown double shot given by that nameless woman. That drink was starting to take me over into a zone but before I was getting ready to give my complaints to *Lucent.* A Brazilian woman walked randomly on my right side holding a platinum-colored rubber held lightly between her teeth. She used her gifted kisser to cover my staff to provide boundaries so that I wouldn't ever have to pull away for any reason.

The enticing Brazilian woman walked away silently as she drifted away a bit while sauntering across the wooden bridge. I then immediately grabbed *Lucent's* right hip with my right hand and filled her *Yoni* with every damn concern I had to administer. My deep breathing begins to become like a light lake fog freed from the golden teeth of the gold grizzly bear's mask. The XL padded Straddle Bench began to babel explosive ruckus of metal rings and chained restraints stroked forward, and back; they hung briefly like the limp tongues of a carnivore in heated thirst. I drummed and marched down her splashing side walk while passing her strong fences, and down into her field of sprinkling systems until I was bathed in her territory. I began to speak to *Lucent* with deep frustration as everyone watched us like a drama play on a fine stage of triple X poetry.

"*Lucent,* I want you to take my entire centerpiece and inner stand that I do not like to be treated trivially in any form. So, take my nucleus and squeeze your moist grip upon my celestial thrust into your fountain of got damn coins of desires, and brutal wishes. Don't fucking ever play with my kindness my petite *Kween*."
Lucent looked back at me thrusting backward against my complaints; her hips declined, and she then squeezed the Straddle Bench tightly. She yelled back at me with nirvana beyond her fluttering eyelids.

"OBERON, I WILL GLADLY TAKE NOTE OF EVERY IN-DEPTH CONCERN YOU HAVE GIVEN, AND I WILL FILE YOUR ISSUES. YES... O' YES, I... WILL!"

With every surge of life that ran from my crown to my root, I felt the most unexplained current of electricity erupting from my core into the burrow of *Lucent's* fruitful *Yoni*. *Lucent* and I attained the greatest convulsions of sacred titillation. That unknown double shot of gold flakes had my eyes seeing things I could not explain. Because I impaled *Lucent's* nature. I watched her divine energy run up and down her spine like techno lights in a rave party of ecstasy. The gold grizzly bear mask begins to feel like it was part of me, at this point I begin feeling the need to roar and growl with certitude. *Lucent's* petite hips started to gyrate against my celestial pole like a mixing bowl, filled with a thick caramel icing held onto my spoon to spread her confectionery-quaking soul.

As my left fingertips strummed her warm bosom my crimson eyes felt inflamed beneath the gold bear mask. The unknown fourth double shot is completely racing through my body with excessive amounts of adrenaline galloping through my blood as my erotic drive increased. I looked up into the ceiling of *The Cage of Glass,* and I saw thousands of small hidden cameras blinking within each of its large glass bars. For a moment I wondered who was watching me step outside of my norm; I just continued to let out my wild and wolf down the divine essence of *Lucent's* hospitality. I knew then that I didn't care if I was being watched while loving on *Lucent's* petite canvas; she was like moving art as we painted time with our every next move made within this *Cage of Glass*. Then out of nowhere, *Lucent* roared out in a growl with trembling salacious words.

"Mmmm...ahh, I believe our meeting of complaints is at its peak of inner standing Oberon. I assure you that the rest of my tour ahead will be much more tastefully agreeable. NOW TAKE MY MIND TO THE FAIRYLAND OF ELATION AND LET'S CUT THE CHITCHAT."

Lucent's words ran through my ears like scorching sunrays of flirtation. She motivates my body to unleash a rupture that would vanquish all doubts that I would ever have within myself. Moments after, my vision got murky and I felt lightheaded; I then began to fall backward off the XL padded Straddle Bench out of *Lucent's* sweetness and back towards the glass floor. As I fell the gold grizzly bear's mask became heavier as the floor got closer to me. Before I made brutal contact with the glass, I heard a small opening beneath me release. I then fell at least 3 feet from *The Cage of Glass* into the deep side of the heated pool. Before I hit the warm water my instincts forced me to grasp a bit of air before I went under. I felt too drained to hold my breath underwater for long, the weight of the mask began pulling me to the bottom, fast!

I was completely submerged in this heated water as I was going down but then I heard loud cheers from all around me in a muffled chant which was odd. I felt the overwhelming feeling to pass out but before that happened, I looked to my right a bit and I saw something extremely dark like the tone of a Black Panther in pursuit. It was a large blurry darkness that hit the water gracefully and swam over to me like a Sailfish cutting the waters. I then begin to lose consciousness. The last thing I felt was my mask being pulled from my head, and two massively soft cushions pressed against the back of my neck. Moments after, I was laid out with my eyes closed and my body fatigued; my head was laying on what I assumed to be the soft thighs of the dark blur that pulled me from the pool. All I could hear around me was live exotic music, and distant mumbles of voices reveling and clicking glasses. I could barely feel what my body was lying on; I assumed I was covered in a large soft towel of cotton. Then the sweet soft voice of the woman's thighs I laid upon began to call out my name as she wisely spoke over my closed eye.

"Oberon, Oberon... wake up! Congratulations monsieur. I would personally like to welcome you as a permanent member of Mrs. Sweet Dame's Nightspot. Your initiation process in The Cage of Glass was quite the performance of erotic elegance. We all enjoyed watching you reach a high level of intimate vandalism with our beautiful sweet Lucent. All here consider "Intimate Vandalism" a top degree of sexual art that embraces the beast-like inner wild of hostility that blocks the balance of peace and chaos. One has to release the unbalanced fury into the universe of a wise Yoni to clear the body of all chaos. It is an intense process that resets the scale of duality when the inner scale has been unaligned on one side of one's

self. Bravo my balanced friend."

I listened to the voice of this woman elatedly speaking to me as I slowly opened my eyes to see her kind plump face. She was a foxy full-figured Senegal woman; her skin tone was like **Black Wolfberries** or **Black Obsidian Stone.** She was wearing an Erotic Lime Green sheer Lace Kimono Kaftan. The sweetness of this woman's energy pulled my attention; I felt dragged in like a ship chain anchored in from the waters to set sail and to be blown by the gust of wind. She was one of the most remarkable plus-size dark chocolates that one could ever wake up to. She then looked down into my eyes to speak over the loud thoughts in my eyes as my mouth remained silent.

"Oberon, everyone around here calls me Zola, and I am also the one who pulled you from the heated pool after you passed out. But that's just a quick reminder if you couldn't remember what happened after you hit the water as hard as you did. Anyhow, everyone here considers me to be the best swimmer in this house of love but furthermore, since you are up now, we can get you dressed. 30 minutes from now Mrs. Dame will be coming out to show us all something special that she has been working on. You do not want to piss her off by not being there in your full mind; definitely after becoming a part of our prestigious "House" of unpredictability. You are now forever a member of Mrs. Sweet Dame's Nightspot, so embrace the abundance of what this place is all about without any judgment."

I then looked up at this remarkably full-bosomed *Kween* to speak my peace as I continued to lie upon her soft thighs of warm jelly; I adored her aroma of rosemary, peppermint, and black pepper.

"Zola, **I thank you for pulling me out of the water beloved. I don't know what the hell happened; the last thing I remember was falling backward out of** *Lucent's* **petite inner thighs. My body then became completely numb all over. I was unable to move my limbs while falling but I felt stronger than I ever felt in my life as I plummeted to the heated pool depth. But** *Zola,* **1 question though. What the hell type of drink did the omniscient woman with the feline eyes give to me?"**

The moment I asked *Zola* that question I then felt my left shoulder regain its feeling as my left shoulder started to sting right after asking about that woman. I then looked under the large soft towel I was in on my left shoulder, and there forever it was; the Grizzly Bear's footprint branded into my skin and sizzling. Before *Zola* answered me, she saw the pain I was in from the branding and decided to tell me something. *Zola's* right eyebrow then rose into an arch and she answered me in a discreet tone; that made me feel like it was forbidden to ask or know anything of what that woman with the feline eyes was about.

"Oberon, you look like a very knowledgeable man, don't be naïve. I am allowed to at least tell you this much with you being permanently part of our sacred "House" now. The one with the feline eyes is a divine woman but yet something more revered; she is considered the Shaman of Mrs. Sweet Dame's Nightspot. The Shaman is always here but unseen on the main floor mostly. She upholds the Nurturing, Receptivity, Guidance, Wisdom, Intuition, and many other arts that I will not convey. What she gave you to drink was only to protect you through the Liberation Ritual to obtain your Intimate Vandalism degree within The Cage of Glass.

The special liquor that you drank was to keep you safe from any heinous spirits trying to attach themselves to you and Lucent; preventing all negative interruptions while in the initiation, all while one indulges in their wild nature. Which makes us what we all are at times as the gold flakes within it act as a symbolic shield. You are shielded to properly release all old attachments and fury that must be removed along with all present spiritual obstacles that are and were to come. The rest of what the Shaman can do should be left alone! With that being said, even Madam Mrs. Dame moves out of the Shaman's path.

There is a deal made between Mrs. Dame and the Shaman; the Shaman must keep this place protected from all nefarious energies that wish to drain out the love we share here, and many other important things required. The Shaman's only rule is that she must never be bothered unless it's a respectful request by Mrs. Dame and for her to never be questioned by anyone, and that deal is never to be broken. Oberon, this place is bigger than a deep sexual release and grand pleasures of many respectable forms but yet a vision to refresh the mind from mental stress. It's a place to fill the body with

96

pure contentment. I believe I just gave you more than enough to inner stand the importance of staying out of the Shaman's way, OK."

On the right of me, I looked up over at **Zola** with **"DAMN"** written all over my face. I was puzzled, that a place like this was located in this area and that **Mrs. Sweet Dame's Nightspot** was seen but unseen to the naked eye of its largely hidden gems beneath it. Beyond my deep thinking, I decided to lift my head from her comfort. As I set my body up looking around, and above me to find out that both of us were relaxing under an emerald green canopy: it was a cream Hammock Hanging Bed with Oakwood bones holding it all together. I then looked to the left of me at **Zola,** she was looking down at me smirking with a light right corner bite of her lip; the swelling of her nipples begins a protrusion from beneath her Erotic Lime Green sheer Lace Kimono Kaftan. My eyes then followed the gaze of her eyes leading me to look at my lap as my meat hung from the towels opening from when I had set up moments ago. I then noticed that all my senses were slowly waking up because I didn't feel a breeze or the warmth upon my staff just yet. **Zola** looked at me and delivered her salacious sarcasm quickly after.

"Oberon, I may be a classy woman but I can be quite the mischievous panther on the roam if you don't put your machinery away. My girl Lucent is no joke but when you deal with me you would never recoup as fast as you are now after The Cage of Glass. I can be peaceful or calm but I rather show you how to ground yourself on my earth and introduce you to my divine authority of my Yoni's clench. But you would require much more rest to deal with one that moves feather lite with the elements of air. Trust Me! But anyways, let's not waste any more time; let's get you back in order my lovely because now we only have 20 minutes before Madam Mrs. Dame comes out from her office lounge."

I then grinned as I looked at **Zola's** desirable reply because I felt that she was not lying about anything; my strength as not fully recovered by far. But if I wasn't so fatigued I damn sure would want some of **Zola's** plump buxom fruits. I replied to her threat or maybe her promise!

"Zola, say less, my seductress love-one. If that offer is still

available after my strength is fully restored to normal! I would gladly let you mount my mountain but just know that you will stutter for breath at a certain altitude as you climb to your demise. So, take your time."

Zola quickly responded while softly cutting off my last word.

"Well Okay Oberon, you talk a great gamble for a strong man who almost drowned but was saved by yours truly; I can tell that you mean what you say and I hold you to that session to prove it. The only thing is that it will be in the room I choose. Now, get your good-looking ass up because the washers are coming by soon to take you to get freshened up."

I then stood up as *Zola* smiled in another direction; a lean gentleman with a silk black cloth over his shoulder was walking her way. He was wearing creased suit pants, bare feet, no shirt, and a burgundy sheer blindfold. He walked up to *Zola* with red wine in a stem glass lotus cup. *Zola* then tilts her head back as he begins gently pouring a small amount into her mouth; the red wine ran down from the line of her bottom lip and glazed over her dolphin tongue ring and out of sight. As she closed her mouth while barely making a sound as she swallowed. The man then takes the silk cloth from his shoulder to dab her come-hitcher lips. Then after, in continued silence, the gentlemen firmly stood at ease next to *Zola* while holding her drink in his right hand. His left hand rested within his left pocket with one thumb positioned outward. I pride myself on being a person who pays attention to my surroundings and details. From seeing all that I have seen, along with the brother's fixed stance, I knew then that this place is strict on rules, discipline, and keeping the chain of command. I assumed at this point that *Zola* must be a high-ranking member here. I then got a tap on my back arm by one of the two mellow mocha women dressed in purple silk robes; I believe that they were the washers here to take me to get clean but before I turned to leave, *Zola* spoke to the women and myself.

"My darling washers, you both look stunning as always, please be quick about getting Oberon cleansed and up to speed, because he now only has 15 minutes to get ready. Madam Mrs. Dame will not allow any members to not be present once she comes into view.

Oberon follow these two women and respect them as you would like to be yourself. But know that they are not mere laborers, they're position is to perform a much more profound cleansing ritual; to give homage to the body for its use as the soul's automobile. Now carry on because we don't have much time."

The two women then responded with a silent head nod to **Zola's** orders, and we began walking; I then nodded with respect and a quick whisper of **"thank you"** to **Zola** once more. While walking away looking back at **Zola,** she smiled at me with a mocking smirk while lying back as she opened her Erotic Lime Green sheer Lace Kimono Kaftan. The silent gentlemen beside her then commenced to kneel in front of her; he began to nimbly pour the red wine from the stemmed glass lotus cup and down between her thighs and along the sides of her **Yoni.** He promptly drank the wine from her earth, and **Zola's** eyes rolled white as her lids batted in bliss; her right hand held his back hairline, pressing his forehead against her **"FUPA."**

As I walked with the two washerwomen while looking back at **Zola,** I then bumped into the back of the two women that I was following. I was confused about the immediate halt when I turned fully towards the ladies in front of me, and I saw that they stopped for this Melanin gentleman up ahead. The tall-built gentlemen wore a **Navy Blue Beret Hat, Navy Blue, and Smokey Gray Scotch Pants, a Blue top with a Smokey Gray trench Pea Coat, and Genuine Smokey Gray Leather Chelsea Boots.** The brother was clean and well put together but had a very dark aura around him as he walked towards us. As the mysterious gentlemen passed by, he kept his head forward and focused; but then he touched the brim of his hat with a slow head nod... giving us a silent greeting.

I thought to myself that this place has a lot of uncanny people passing through here, and it kept getting weirder the longer I was here. Then one of the washers looked at my unsettled face, and she then broke her silence to tell me what that strange dark aura was that just passed by us.

"Well Oberon, I can tell you this, that eccentrically malicious man is named Grievous aka Uptown Cannibal, Sister Sovereign is his wife and they both own a well-known place called "The Serenaders

Lounge" and they're involved in many other powerful dealings. But trust and believe, the "Denmarc Family Bloodline" is not a family that you want to piss off or ever attempt to waste their time. Beyond people fearing him and his family, Mr. Grievous is a big-hearted gentleman, and he and his family physically keep Mrs. Sweet Dame's Nightspot marked as sacred ground. This place is also under the protection of Mr. Grievous, he has an agreement with Mrs. Dame just as the Shaman Kween does.

Mr. Grievous and the Shaman Kween agreed to never step wrong on each other's path and to always remain courteous. Mr. Grievous had only one rule of three things as a whole, which was for Madam Mrs. Dame to only purchase her Wine, Liquor, and Antiques from him. In return, He vowed to her that she would always be protected with all of what she did even after his death; as long as it made sense and it was just. Furthermore, Oberon, now you only have 10 minutes for us to get your body back right but it won't take us long to do what we have to do. Definitely with the two of us handling you... so, let us proceed."

I then looked far behind me while looking at all that stood, conversing, and carousing; regardless of all the conglomerating, the people urgently cleared the path of **Mr. Grievous** while they nervously greeted him with mild head nods of respect. As he walked through silently, casting a grim shadow under the flashing lights unceasingly. **Mr. Grievous** walked towards the exit and up to the long gold-lined center of steps; once reaching the top the vault door opened and the **superior receptionist Iguana** walked out the vault door holding something. She then briefly talked with **Mr. Grievous** before seeing him off; once the talking ceased, **Iguana** handed him a swollen Leather Satchel. **Iguana** then shook his hand with a smile, and he kissed her cheek as he walked out; the vault door closed soon after his exit. Certainty then hit me hard once again; I knew that I was now part of something that could probably end my life but only if I were to speak about anything of this place outside these walls or those within it. But I was already accepting this place as a second home, and I valued the membership up to this point; my loyalty is now set beyond my unwanted gravestone.

The two women then pulled me out of my deep thoughts and towards our destination as I held my large towel tight around me. I still felt a bit light-headed from the fall into the water but I walked firmly behind the ladies to get cleaned up. After a couple of minutes of being showered down quickly by their graceful hands I only had two minutes to get dressed, and back out to the poolside. All three of us dried off our bodies, and quickly oiled up; the oil had the scent of lavender and rosemary. I then gazed at the two women with their backs turned in front of me, as they placed silver linen robes around their naked coffee silk flesh. Their robes had a large grizzly bear's foot embroidered on the back of its center. I then felt the sizzling again once I saw the symbol of the bear's foot burned in my skin but the feeling went as fast as it came. One of the women then handed me the same style of robe. As I placed it upon me, It fit perfectly; the fabric felt good on my bareness. Then one of the women spoke quickly.

"Oberon, you are indisputably handsome enough for one to need a taste of but you are wasting valuable time in which we don't have. We all have to get to the poolside right the hell now; I do not want Madam Mrs. Dame to punish me for being late again. My Yoni and ass are still hurting; Madam Mrs. Dame was pissed; I got punished by her paddling and her Thigh Spreader Bar last time... just for dropping a bucket of ice on her office Oakwood floor. If you think Meeka was insane and over the top, wait until you piss off Madam Mrs. Dame; she makes Meeka look mild compared to her. Anyways, we gotta go... like now!"

All three of us rushed out of the swinging doors of the cleansing room to the poolside with only seconds to spare. The two women then smiled at me and told me to wait there as they rushed away towards their next obligation. I stood by the poolside in the center next to the end of the long glass bar while admiring the new feel of the vast room. No one was in the heated pool, and the color of this place was now a glim hue of dim peach mood lights with a rhythmic flicker upon them. There was also a massive platform made of the thickest glass I have ever seen, the platform extended out and over half of the heated pool towards the end at its warm middle.

The pool seemed to be releasing a thicker and higher rising of steam than what it was before I went to be cleansed. Next to the platform was a wide stage of live musicians, which had been serenading us all night.

They were moving around the stage like a turn table of vinyl. This has to be the first time I heard the live music not playing anything. I could only assume that they were switching out the band members for breaks as the new group got ready for whatever this big moment was about to be. Beyond all that, various royal blue lights were beaming down on this platform; the lighting shined onto its transparency down into the pool floor. Royal blue lights reached from the bottom of the heated pool, and beamed upwards but slightly dimmer. It looked like it was about to be a show like one as never seen.

As I stood there contemplating this room's mood gradually changing into something more romantically bound. Then I smelled a familiar scent creeping over my shoulders along with the sweet sound of *Lucent's* voice. Her soft hands quickly reached around my waist from the back of me onto my front; she held my robes peeping growth from under my silver linens center as she spoke to my roaming mind.

"Don't turn around Oberon, just let my hands speak the greatest language of palm stroking your print, and let me translate your immense scroll of long hieroglyphs to consummate. Oh Yes Papi, let me heave. Ha-ha... Mmmmmm, we definitely reached a level inside "The Cage of Glass" my love. I honored every moment of us, now you are forever aligned with Mrs. Sweet Dame's Nightspot. Anyhow, I have to get back to work and don't say anything back when I release my hands from your root. Just let your eyes watch me sashay away into the lights within my divine feminine. See you later my royal loveliness, and enjoy the show handsome!"

As *Lucent* released her grip and tiptoed around to my left shoulder on her tips; she pulled my left shoulder robe off a bit and gently kissed my branded bear's foot. *Lucent* walked away in her new uniform but the same style from earlier, a work vest and her petite body unclothed beautifully. As she sashayed away, I could still feel her bent over *Yoni* split, warmly taking my banana with her grip into her realm of eruptions, moans, and a twist of her fit and dainty hips. Then all of a sudden, the drummer sticks began to slowly double-tap the Hi-hats, Snares, and Bass Pedal. Everyone then became completely quiet holding their drinks, smoking their smoke and no one had a whisper. Everybody just relaxed on the hammock beds, the poolside seats at the table, or the leather couch that ran along each wall within the shadows.

As I looked around the massive room I spotted a gold reserved sign at a table with my name in reflective silver calligraphy. This table was poolside in front of the glass platform of royal blue lights with my chair facing the platform. So, I headed over to my table as the lady drummer drummed and gave the sticks her full control. The gentleman fingered the keys of the Grand Piano wearing a blue silk blindfold; The Violins Bow begins to seesaw upon the strings making her melody moan and scream. The Harp player leaned her Soundbox upon her right shoulder and caressed the cords towards its pillar and back against her heart. I mean this music was forcefully passionate; I just sat in my chair and vibed out to the music.

Then a waiter walked up to me placing a bronze tray upon my table and walked away in silence. Upon it was a joint, an ashtray, a gold lighter with a new bottle of tequila with a shot glass, and a letter with a message that read.

"Much love and salutations Oberon, I send honor to your journey of facing your inner wild and inner peace; always respect your duality, and keep the balance of life. You are now part of many that walk as one conglomerate. You are always safe here unless you force the opposite and betray this house. You will learn the rules of this chamber soon, so just enjoy yourself, Sincerely, Madam Mrs. Dame."

All I could do was grin with certainty because I overstood every word written, and I honored it. I then cracked open my drink and took three hard shots to the head; I sparked my joint and let the smoke roll off to the wet of my tongue blowing the smoke off to the right of me. The live band played erotically behind me to my far right as my bare foot tapped against the floor. After a while I began to wonder why we rushed out here and nothing had started; so, I assumed it was to keep all of us on our toes. But then an indoor snow machine started releasing snowflakes from the ceiling over the glass platform. I watched them quickly melt against the floor of the warm platform's glass. I thought to myself, either I was too high or this place was still testing the boundaries of my mind.

I looked behind me a couple of tables over to see *Zola* lying down where we were earlier. *Zola* was relaxed with her legs crossed holding her drink in her left hand; we then made eye contact and **Zola** winked at me. **Zola** raised her right hand and pointed at the glass platform as if I was about to miss something. Then that beautiful loud bird whistle from earlier was heard all over but louder. The band begins to perform stronger, and sexier. Everyone raised their glasses high in silence while biting their lips, and rocking their head to the subtle melody of the live music. The whole room looked to the end of the glass platform; as the snowflakes fell softly from the ceiling, disappearing onto its warm clearness. Then an intense sound of a grizzly bear roared with a deep huffed growl; the deep rumbling came from behind two tall Black Crushed Velvet Drapes that hung from the ceiling at the end of the glass platform. I was too high and relaxed to respond abruptly but my guard was up, I thought to myself that there's no way in hell a real Grizzly Bear could be down here in this place. But at this point, I knew that this establishment was unpredictable!

For some reason after hearing the roar of the wild, I then felt the need to stand up after all my thoughts rambled in my skull. I watched as the entire room stood as if we all held the same idea. I held my joint and took in deep puffs of anxiousness, and then the large drapes opened, and the music became even more seductive. Then out walked a humongous Grizzly Bear onto the platform, roaring like it was saluting **Madam Mrs. Dame** as she set upon its back. The Grizzly Bear walked out slowly as snowflakes fell and dissolved against her skin; the flakes of snow settled softly upon the Grizzly Bear's thick brown fur. I immediately dropped my joint in the ashtray, I couldn't believe the shit I was seeing right now. I then grabbed my bottle of Tequila from the table and gulped down some spirits as I marveled at this breathtaking moment. How the hell was this even possible, all of this just from me taking a ride out from my house; to randomly find this place within all its raw lavishness!

Then the Grizzly Bear growled one last time before it stopped in the center of the platform; it slowly began to lie down on its belly for **Madam Mrs. Dame** to be removed from it. Then out walked a very tall shirtless dark brute with a solid keg. This guy was wearing the same type of Grizzly Bear Mask I wore with **Lucent.** He only had on that mask, tan army-fatigued pants, and black boots. As he walked towards **Madam Mrs. Dame** and took her from the top of the Grizzly Bear carefully into his arms; He carried her down onto the glass platform, and gently upon her bare feet, and he then exited soon after.

Madam Mrs. Dame stood in front of her Grizzly Bear as it closed its eyes and slept behind her. She raised her left hand to the sky, and everyone immediately began to take their seats to embrace her long-awaited performance. The room was buzzing high like wild hornets waiting to catch their prey; they sat dormant yet calmly waiting to endure the raw nectar of *Madam Mrs. Dame's* sweetest energy.

Madam Mrs. Dame's oiled skin was like a finely carved dark chocolate, moist and shining above this heated pool as the cold flakes of snow kept her within a balanced temp of comfort. Her War-Locs hung from her crown as medallions of gold radiated from her crown Locs length. She then held both her hands high in suspense above her War-Locs spreading her fingerprints nimbly; her hands whirled as she caressed the cold flakes of the falling snow that touched the tone of her lubricated obsidian flesh. She wore a Leather Open Breast Full Body Harness and a bottom Lingerie Set with a Leather Choker Chain Necklace.

Madam Mrs. Dame was superbly well-proportioned with plump breasts which complemented the harness itself. I loved watching the cold flakes of snow motivating her gumdrops to become protrusive; she danced with a furious poker face while looking at the ceiling. The entire room was enchanted by her careless ways within a room of sprung eyes. As I set, I leaned forward, smitten by her stance as I set near her divine vitality; so, I honored this moment and set comfortably back against my chair. I wrote all of *Madam Mrs. Dame's* beauty in the scroll of my eyes and read her every move like a teller of fortunes and considerable pleasure to come.

I leaned my head to the right a bit, watching *Madam Mrs. Dame* as she blew the snowflakes away with a single kiss into the air. I watched her warm breath release briefly from her black cherry lips, just like a forest fog at the brink of a cold night wind. I then became rendered by her dance along with everyone else in the room; we all became a bit motionless and struck with a profound silence.

I thought to myself, all the *Kweens* here are of great flavor for one to respect but *Madam Mrs. Dame* has shown me why she is the leader of this hidden place, and the reason she is loved as well as feared. *Madam Mrs. Dame* then slowly raised her right hand upon her oiled fit belly. She quickly spread her black cherry fingernails onto her skin like a Japanese War Fan. Her right hand pressed firmly against her stomach, right against the large tribal tattoo of a Grizzly Bear's claw along with powerful symbols circling its art. Her left hand remained twirling gracefully above her mind as she stepped forward with her right leg crossing her calf over to her left shin tightly. *Madam Mrs. Dame* then closed her gray and hazel eyes just a little as her pupils furled backward into her upper lids. She begins to roll her hips in a fast yet slow bewitching fashion as my vision becomes triggered and trapped by her passionate illusion.

Snowflakes began to melt, around and upon her body, cooling her off as the heated pool released warmth which kept her toasty; such a balance to be respected. I felt so damn serene in this moment while watching *Madam Mrs. Dame's* sultry movements becoming a reward to my thoughts. It was like a spiritual waltz as my eyes whirled with her every move while feeling the live music from the band flowing through my blood. I was vibing out hard as the seductive music never seemed to clash with the *Madam's* motions, almost as if the rhythm of the instruments were married to the frequency of her hips as the tense sounds played as one. The more I stared I felt my plum tree swelling under my root as her hips dropped to each side gracefully along with each hit of the snares. *Madam Mrs. Dame's* tight belly begins to roll in a wave as she bounces her thick cuffed foundation. She rattled her tail end with every vibration of each pound of the drummer's kick pedal ramming the batter head with force.

Then my tongue licked out across my closed lips like an old-fashioned typewriter reaching its paper typing edge, and scaling back to the right to press that ink against the next desired line. Her toes tapped the glass platform in cadence with the groove of the Hi-Hats and Cymbals. Damn, this woman hasn't gone into her full dance yet and her body is already telling me a deep story without one word given.

I had to hold my print pressed against my stomach as my robe truly hid nothing thus far. As I watched *Madam Mrs. Dame,* her hips moved like two serpents striking their meal from both sides; she danced this exotic ballet of yoga like no other. With her legs still crossed and her waist moving in small rotation, she bent down to the glass platform placing both her hands flat to the stage with gentle sways of allurement. Her palms pressed hard to the glass and her War-Locs fell to the translucent floor between her toned oiled arms. The strength in her figure raised her entire body in the air upside down; her head moved from side to side like rare vines in a tropical storm. She reformed the minds of this vast room of passionate people, placing us all in a zone to be entertained beyond our thoughts. We all watched the voluptuous cuffs of her cheeks become juicy and wide, as she unclenched her legs and positioned her thighs to decline in the air. *Madam Mrs. Dame* bent her knees out to her sides; she flattened the bottom of her feet to meet together in meditation as the gold dolphins on her toe ring shined with the room's lights.

The *Madam* began to deeply rotate her hips in the ambiance as her beautiful dark chocolate assets took my deception of time. I valued her balance and flexible property as she performs with an agenda within her aura. Her energy shifted my desires as I watched her *Yoni* split under her bottom lingerie set to twelve and six o'clock; her arms held down a position of a seven and five's point of time to play. I loved the way she wore her set… that sexy Full Body Leather and Open Breast Harness with an elegant bottom of lingerie; she made my hands tingle with an urge to hold her and unwrap this royal *Kween* from her harness of leather. Beyond all my thoughts and my palms becoming eagerly wetter and wondering what was next. I forced my passion to rest as *Madam Mrs. Dame* continued to sway upside down; she danced like the crown of a snake being called out by my flute music of melodic riffs from beneath my robe's hard print of drumming veins.

I became captured by the *Madams* dance while those around and nearby looked to be in the same condition as I was. While my sight wandered toward another delight coming up to me on my right peripheral. This woman was another eye-opening sweetness, an Amazon woman who stood at *7'0"* feet tall; she was gracefully gliding my way. This Brazilian *Kween* wore a name tag reading *Slender'Guava;* this waitress approached me with a sweet yet calm expression on her face. Her long silk-like hair of wavy curls ran down her beautiful lean elevation, flowing just about the mid-thigh length of her body. She wore a transparent Lace Peacock Teal loose-fit suit and Lace Barefoot Crochet Sandals. I truly admired the creativity in this place when it came to the attire and innovation.

As **Madam Mrs. Dame** danced her dance, I slightly looked up to my right towards *Slender-Guava.* Within her right hand, she held a copper bowl of vanilla bean Ice cream with thin sliced strawberries; but this dessert dish was without a spoon to retrieve its sweetness. I felt so high out of my mind and I was actually in need of a treat. When I tried to reach for the bowl, then out of the blue, *Slender'Guava* struck my right grip of knuckles with a Chestnut Brown Leather Spanking Strap with her left hand. I then had a recollection of all the shit that I've gone through already and was not about to keep getting struck for no damn reason. Before getting infuriated, 3 very bright peach mood lights shined from above, directly over *Slender'Guava* and me; confusion set in once more. I looked back over at **Madam Mrs. Dame,** and she was standing upright as she danced leisurely; the **Madam** was cutting me with a gaze of sensual harshness and hostility. I then got more grounded within my humility and relaxed but I wondered why **Madam Mrs. Dame** looked at me with so much anger. I was also still at a loss for why *Slender'Guava* struck my hand.

I was perplexed while the live music played on as the people around me acted odd as if they knew something that I did not. I then said fuck it and stood up; the lights beamed down over my table yet putting me into another unnecessary spotlight of attention. Then a wooden ramp was released from the ceiling, which led from **The Glass Platform,** and over the heated pool upon the floor near my table. *Slender'Guava* stood tall over me holding the copper bowl of vanilla bean Ice cream and thinly sliced strawberries. She then stepped to the side of the ramp and pointed for me to go over the wooden ramp that led to **Madam Mrs. Dame's** dark dance of beauty as she waited. The room then screamed, whistled, and clapped in applause for another round of amusement at my damn expense, which pissed me off but also felt becoming at the same time.

I thought to myself, *"This was some bullshit, but there is no turning back... for any reason."* So, I snatched the bottle of tequila from the table by its neck and took some gulps, and I slammed it down on the table annoyed; I then made my move. I then walked over to the wooden ramp but before I walked over the ramp *Slender'Guava* stood there holding her left hand out to me. Finally breaking her silence, she sweetly spoke with four polite words, ***"Oberon, your robe please!"*** I looked at this remarkable tall woman within her teasing eyes as she stood in her transparent Peacock Teal Lace Suit. ***Slender'Guava*** waited for me to concede as she waited with her fruitful 34C cups and bare-skinned body posed behind her sheer clothing; she has such a contour to cherish.

With the taste of tequila coating my tongue and mouth, I swallowed the remaining taste of liquor that lingered within my jawline. I faced the wooden ramp as **Madam Mrs. Dame** danced in front of her sleeping Grizzly Bear in a pleasing trance. I removed my robe and handed it over to **Slender'Guava,** and the weight of my passion balled up into a fine knot within my chest. As I was about to walk away, **Slender'Guava** slapped my right ass cheek; I grunted in anger but then she told me in a serious tone as I stood there naked.

"Oberon, my love… Do not speak or approach the Madam once you have reached The Glass Platform! Your only goal is to take the sweet treat in this copper bowl to Madam Mrs. Dame's Grizzly Bear. All you have to do is place the copper bowl down by its sleeping mouth and wait for your answer. If the Grizzly Bear licks the bowl clean and leaves you unharmed, then you are worthy for the next step, and only then you can approach the Madam but mindfully."

Granted that your approach goes well, you will then be given the Grizzly Bears ancestral name and then you will gain full approval or refusal by Madam Mrs. Dame. If the Grizzly Bear feels that you are unworthy and it smells the wrong energy from you then you will be its rations for today. You will be considered a gift to one of our ancestors of nature regardless if you took the sacred mark burned into your flesh or not."

I looked at **Slender'Guava** as I then bit down on my lip a little as extreme anxiety sets in; after being told to perform such a random act of craziness, just for me to prove my loyalty. I then forced myself to relax and respond to her calmly in an undertone.

"Slender'Guava, I thought I was already part of the family after the other initiation trials with *Lucent* and the *Shaman Kween*! I even got marked with the Grizzly Bears claw; I already went

through many tasks along with much-unneeded disrespect from *Meeka's* **crazy ass. So why the hell do I have to feed** *Madam Mrs.* *Dame's* **got damn murderous pet?"**

While speaking, the branded Grizzly Bear's foot began to painfully burn on my shoulder; it burned more, every time I questioned the oddness of this place's traditions. *Slender'Guava* then responded with a tone of haste in her sexy voice.

"Oberon, you are not in the place to know certain things yet, I'm sure the Shaman already warned you of that. Oberon just because somebody told you that your loyalty is done being tested does not mean that your dedication can not be challenged after... remember that. Be on point at all times, and get your handsome ass up there before the Madam hurt us both for ignoring her presence with so much hesitation. Also, please do not drop one creamy drip from the copper bowl, it's considered a sign of ultimate disrespect so please be careful."

I then over stood clearly as I nodded my head to her with a deep breath of irritation following after. I then took the copper bowl from *Slender'Guava* as this *7'0"* foot Amazon beauty bends down, and kissed the right side of my neck to gift me with a smooch of protection. *Slender'Guava* deliciously walked away towards the live band to watch everything from the left side of the stage from afar.

The guest looked towards me roaring with cheers of an audience waiting for the bloodshed of a warrior going into a ring of beasts. I then tuned out everything around me as I tightly held the copper bowl of melted ice cream and thinly sliced strawberries, I walked up and across the wooden ramp cautiously. I looked ahead of me at *Madam Mrs. Dame* erotically dancing; the radiance within her movements dazzled unbreakable energy throughout her saucy aura.

Madam Mrs. Dame's Grizzly Bear continued to sleep in a deep slumber over all the loud music, voices chanting, and cheering. The *Madam* remained in a dancing trance as she filled the room with her tasteful performance. I walked halfway over the wooden ramp feeling the warm intensity of the pool once more but above it; at the same time, I felt the cold snowflakes that fell from the ceiling onto every muscle of my stride.

The senses of my flesh were confused about whether it wanted me to have goosebumps or have my pores release my sweat. The hot and cold sensation together was like a chill that one would receive when stepping out from a hot shower, and into a space of cold central air. Along with the warmth of the heated pool is a hell of an experience when it hits you at once. Beyond that, the closer I got to the end of the wooden ramp towards *The Glass Platform,* I then felt the ferocity of *Madam Mrs. Dame's* energy immensely. The *Madam's* aura was impressive. Her beauty was damn sure created with patience as well as many of the other wonderful women here tonight.

Furthermore, the closer I got, I felt even more tense as my feet pressed forward against the wooden surface leading me to *The Glass Platform.* It also seemed as if the Grizzly Bear slept deeply but yet patiently waiting on me to feed its sharp sweet tooth. The Grizzly Bear continued to breathe heavily in slumber; my legs felt like wet chard lumber when I stepped forward. I took heed to the live melodious music that complimented the rhythmic hips of *Madam Mrs. Dame's* Belly dancing; her waist ascended and descended in a beautiful gyration. The divine constellation of her luminary body blazed with vivid soul palettes. Firmly continuing forward but attentive while hoping to not spill a drip from this copper bowl of a sweet melt becoming more of a milkshake of plunged fruit. Beyond all of that, while walking naked I felt more of the room's profound ambiance; the loud applause became murmuring cheers from the shadows of the lights reach as all discussions became a muffled distance.

I stepped off the wooden ramp onto *The Glass Platform,* and without delay the guest went silent as my bare feet touched the glass. But I maintained my peripheral focus on the *Madam* as she danced superbly ahead of me on my right. The music played lustfully as it had all night; I felt the music vibrating within my chest. The Grizzly Bear remained unpredictable as it slept. I took a deep breath and stepped past the visual enchantment of the *Madam's* dance and towards this unwavering lounging beast.

I then felt the eyes of *Madam Mrs. Dame* burning through me as I passed by her as she continued her erotic dance of fury. With caution,

I respectfully stood before this slumbering beastly being with a furry skull that was larger than my chest. The muscled shoulder hump of this Grizzly Bear rose up and down as it breathed deeply in its rest. Its claws were long, sharp, and curved as its colossal paws rested on *The Glass Platform's* warm transparency; I believe this beast was patiently waiting to decide my fate.

As I stood with every part of me dressed in nothing but the copper bowl that I held for this deadly moment of approval or denial. I knew like hell I didn't want to be slaughtered just for trying to chill in *Mrs. Sweet Dame's Nightspot* but it was too late to change my mind. I then looked around the room as the snowflakes melted down against my skin's warmness and onto the copper bowl cream and fruit slices. I held the bowl down against my shift to protect my pipeline as it hung.

I filled my lungs with the sweet aroma in the atmosphere as I breathed hard with anxiety. The band's live music begins to play lewdly lower to allow the female saxophonist to riddle sumptuous notes of rose gold Sax melodies. Her wind blew sheet music like leaves teetering from a branch after the coming and going of a rainstorm. I then assumed it was an intentional indication of my dilemma to calm my tenseness; I stood ready for whatever my fate was.

The melodic elements of the saxophonist playing made me less agitated, and I relaxed a bit; I then kneeled slowly to my knees before the Grizzly Bears closed my eyes. As my knees pressed down on the glass my body became calmer; I then placed the copper bowl down on *The Glass Platform.* But soon after I placed the dish down *Madam Mrs. Dame* instantly stopped dancing. The *Madam* kneeled towards the audience with her beautiful backside of dark chocolate and bottom thickness set within my right peripheral. Her cuff line cheeks pressed upon her calf, Achilles tendon, and the heel of her feet. *Madam Mrs. Dame* then raised her hands to the glaring lights; she began twiddling her fingers in the fall of snowflakes. My knees, shins and midfoot both pressed against the glass harder with uneasiness; no matter what I felt or did my eyes remained locked and centered on this Grizzly Bears movement.

While kneeled still, my nose was stuck with the close smell of melted vanilla bean Ice cream and thin sliced strawberries; other than the scent that came from the copper bowl, the breath of the Grizzly Bear reeked of honey and seasoned meat. While the music played and the room's anticipation grew in whispers; **Madam Mrs. Dame** set in a calm trance with her hand in the air catching snowflakes as they gracefully fell towards her. I couldn't believe I was kneeling naked with just a copper bowl between myself and this Grizzly Bear; it felt like forever waiting for its response to the offering. I then blinked once and quickly felt the heat of the pool increase; it was like a mild furnace from under the glass. I blinked a second time, and the snowflakes that fell began to come down more like confetti of melting snow. But when I closed my lids to blink the third time my hands were gripping the top of my thigh muscles while wondering what was next; as my eyes opened, I felt the illusion of time become still after what I saw!

I couldn't believe that this beast was now standing at least 10 feet over me and with the copper bowl full and untouched. I didn't even hear it when it woke up to even move to stand; it then looked down at me with contemplation in one eye and ingest in the other. This Grizzly Bear was unlike any I had ever seen, I had the urge to look away and sprint out of this place but my body didn't want to budge. The Grizzly Bear just stood over me without any reaction while continuing to look down into my sight like it was hunting for information through the eyes of my soul. My nose flared with fury as I got ready for what was coming next with the gut feeling that I fucked up coming here.

Then I looked over the shoulder of the Grizzly Bear, and I noticed up high on a center balcony stood the **Shaman Kween** standing in her Turquoise Egyptian Cutout dress with an exotic Lace Masquerade Mask upon her face. Her spellbinding feline eyes shimmered with the lights near the shadows of the balcony's edge; then the Grizzly's branded footprint upon me began to sizzle more intensely. The Grizzly Bear then made another move while it stood high with its head pointed up to the snowflakes falling, and the deep roar that it released made my body numb. The snowflakes fell over its body like a mild blizzard, and down into the mouth of its forever sharpness with its arms hanging and claws growling loudly.

The Grizzly Bear came down on all fours heavy against the glass and leaned over to me as it stood over the Copper Bowl; its large head was now hovering above my branded shoulder dreadfully bellowing near my right ear. I couldn't move not one part of my body but for some reason, I felt unbothered as it stood near me roaring. Out of the blue, The Grizzly Bear became silent as it sniffed deeply at it and stepped back a bit to lick the bear's foot branded on my flesh; then for some reason, the burning sizzle went away completely.

The Grizzly Bear stepped back further from me stretching out on its belly in front of the Copper Bowl and licked it clean in seconds; the large Grizzly lay on its side and went back to sleep. Then, and only then I learned the ancestral name of this Grizzly Bear; I looked to its ear at the words engraved in a solid gold piece pierced on the Grizzly Bears ear with the name reading... *"Prudence."*

I looked back towards the balcony where the Shaman no longer stood, and I took a deep breath looking up to the cold snowflakes plummeting down. I repeated the name of the Grizzly Bear to myself out loud once more shaking my head in thought, thinking of all the recent debauchery, and the things that I had experienced.

"The ancestral name of the Grizzly Bear... is... *Prudence!* **Damn, this shit crazy!"**

While I contemplated on the name, the entire room began to give me a standing ovation; I assumed the cheers were for me not becoming supper for their roaring forest totem that could have ended my life instantly. I then stood up slowly from **The Glass Platform** with my naked body feeling vigorous, my hand was tightly balled into a fist at my sides; I held my head high while feeling refreshed and unconfined. I looked around the room at all the cheering faces. Within the crowd, I spotted all the women I met tonight in which I valued the deep conversations along with the enticing encounters that I had with them. The women I got close to winked at me clapping. I watched all of the half-filled glasses held high, giving homage to me for taking a gamble with my life to be part of this sacred place of high-level courting. My thoughts were severed by the rigorously provocative voice of **Madam Mrs. Dame** ripping and slicing through everything that made a sound in **Mrs. Sweet Dame's Nightspot;** the **Madam** began to slowly stand with her back turned towards me and her pet Grizzly Bear. The live music stopped and the room went silent, you could only hear the breathing of every guest in the room and your thoughts. The **Madam** spoke loudly while never turning around to me as she spoke at me.

"Oberon, as I enunciate observations... You will stand there and not speak until I am heard. Know this, you still have to be given my last words upon your completion towards being part of me, and the grandness of this house. Consider this large room a vast terrarium in an infinite house of people that are like my mixed garden of fresh fruits and rare flowers. Overstand, that my fruits are meant to be ate out of its sustenance while slowly allowing one's palate to encourage the burst of its central flavors. My vegetables are meant to be sucked gently to stimulate their core to release all of its vitamins gradually from the inside.

All of my flowers are the beautiful healing factors of those that respect my wrath, love, and worth... they work for and alongside me, for life; my flowers can be harmless or harmful when required to be, upon my decree. You know my flowers well don't you, Mr. Oberon! Did you love my roses of hibiscus, lilies, and so forth that allowed you entry into my home and between their leaves? I watched you from my hidden cameras as you made your way from the first level of the front door, and down a level before the vault. You have met most of my flowers, like the ones that examined, informed, guided, toughened, rescued, and washed your tight ass and then some.

You get my point, I'M SURE OF IT! My question to you is, what would you be considered as within my serene garden of growth, love, and pleasure? Before you answer, know that I do not accept weeds that do not hold healing qualities, nor do I accept pests of any kind trying to destroy what I have built; I despise thieves that steal from my garden without at least stealing for me first. Know that I am the sun, water, soil, and the only main gardener that keeps this orchard healthy and flourishing. So, Oberon, please don't be predictable or sarcastic and say that you are the gardening tool because what would I need with a garden hoe in a place where only powerful hands and grounded instruments of love should embrace wealthy soil to motivate its true fulfillment? YOU NOW MAY ANSWER, IF YOU ARE ABLE!"

As **Madam Mrs. Dame** stood across from me, I just looked at her as she faced the crowd with her back toward me ever so enticingly palatable to fondle. I decided to answer the **Madam** truthfully with hopes of reviving the dead silence in the vast room back to its normal motions of titillating noise.

"With all due respect, *Madam Mrs. Dame,* whether my answer mattered to you or not, just like yourself… I to will give only so much of myself towards my desires until I have reached my boundary. I have been taking risks out of joy within my curiosity this entire night. I stand here with my bare body and my manhood stretched and pulsating and yet I now am questioned as to what I am considered as in your garden.

Beloved, I stumbled along this place not reaching for anything special. I planned to have a drink and some good-ass conversation with ravishing women like yourself. Yet I was given way more than I was used to from some of the wonderful *Kweens* I encountered which took me to great heights. *Madam*, what I am trying to say to you is that I wouldn't consider myself anything within your garden at this point; but you could now know me as a dark fucking rain cloud passing through to wet your unyielding field. If you would allow me to be the balance of shade over the bed of some of your feminine flowers that need a break from your sunbath of beautiful radiation; THEN I WILL!

If not, let me just marvel at the way you garden, to learn your land, to earn your waters, and to know the way you shine even for a moment. I am no garden tool but I am a durable force once motivated by a *Kween* who may want me as I may her; so, what now… *Madam*?"

Mrs. Dame remained quiet after I spoke, the room locked their eyes on the *Madam* while waiting for her response as I was. After a minute or so, she turned around to me and snapped her fingers at the band to play her favorite song without telling them with words. *Madam Mrs. Dame* looked back at me with a sexy sneer of demining words loudly with sarcasm.

"Oberon, the decision of Prudence is important to me but I am still the last word of approval; I guess your answer has made my Yoni a bit feverish and entertained by your clever arrogance. Oberon, you

are now substantially a new breath of divine wind to my night spot. I will now reward you with a short ritual dance of completion. Unclench your tense fist and lean your back against the fur of Prudence, and know that you will never be harmed by our Grizzly Bear unless I demand so. We are one now, and you are my possession as they are but not in the way that you might assume. So, rest your formidable backside against Prudence and receive the edible oils and herbs that I have prepared. Let my oils decline down the flex and flesh of your brawn; let it be poured over the black line of your ganja-burned lips, and down to your neck and then the rest."

The body language of **Madam Mrs. Dame** felt more relaxed towards me than she had a moment ago. So, I just moved forward in silence as the live band up the tempo to something smooth, and soulful for the **Madam's** dance ritual of completion. The room began holding up burning smoky gray and gold stripe candles in the air; they all were bobbing their heads back and forth to the tranquil music. As I stepped to the side of **Prudence,** I turned my back to the sleeping beast and laid my naked body against its fur full of cold melting snowflakes. I felt a strong chill through my body as the snowflakes dissolved against me, and my full backside was pressed against the Grizzly bear's soft thick fur. The melted snow ran down my gluteal cleft between my legs and dripped from my secured spheres swimming with my creamy gelato.

Prudence then took a deep breathing huff and continued sleeping as I lay against its deep-furred body; the burning candles around the heated pool were like fluttering fireflies trapped in a mason jar with a lid of poked holes. **Madam Mrs. Dames** stood a couple of feet from me with her legs together; her hands were pressed to each other and pointing down in front of her breast like she was waiting for something to happen.

The **Madam** stood there waiting with her hands now open together and outward as she stared down into her palms. I leered to my right as the curvaceous **Shaman Kween** walked out from the shadows across the wooden ramp towards **Madam Mrs. Dame;** the **Shaman** was holding a Brass Singing Bowl full of the edible oils and herbs that I was told about by the **Madam**. I looked over at **Madam Mrs. Dame** as she looked over at me. She was puckering her black cherry lips as she stood in a position like a statue with her hands open. The **Shaman** then approached the **Madam** at her left side, and suddenly the **Shaman** looked instantly over at me while she stood there within her divine feminine with a look of mastery. All I could do was relax and admire the snowflakes falling between our paths of sight.

The feline eyes of this beguiling **Shaman Kween** became murky while shining along with the room lights murmuring the sounds of dim bulbs surging with mild wattage. The **Shaman** looked back towards the **Madam** and gently placed the Brass Singing Bowl in her hands; she then turned away from the **Madam** to gaze back at me once more. The **Shaman Kween** began to walk my way with this sort of ship sailing glide in her motion. The **Shaman** approached my bare body with such a transcendent aura; she stood in my nearness placing the back of her right hand on top of my branded skin, it was stinging while near the energy of her supremeness.

I watched the back of her hand slithering over the sizzling healing of the Grizzly Bear's paw burned into my flesh; she lifted my right hand from the grizzly's plush fur with reason within her feline eyes. The **Shaman** looked at me within the depth of my perception; she slowly slid the mid-knuckles of my fingers between her warm legs and beyond her exotic cutout attire of garments. The **Shaman** pressed my right hand against her **Yoni** firmly, and I breathed deeply with awareness of her being… gracefully tempting my cognitive abilities.

Then there was a sudden whiff of fresh Papaya that lingered from her **Yoni** as she sweetened the mid-knuckles of my fingers with her eminent nectar. The room watched patiently as the **Shaman** whispered a beautiful language of which I'd never heard. She then became silent moments after she gifted my eardrum with refined words that she had spoken; she then leaned back to look through my eyes. Without ever moving her lips to speak, the **Shaman** then spoke into my mind, **"Let the pain be as if it wasn't… fore I am ever potent and untamable by any or all."** Staring at me with her remarkable feline eyes the mystic woman slid my rested right hand from against her tight soaked **Yoni**.

She continued to speak in my mind as she told me to lick her fresh nectar of drips falling from my knuckles without having any disbelief of her reason. I looked down at my right hand and slowly licked her

Papaya juices from my back fingers; I would consider her natural sweetness very tasteful upon my tongue like none other. She then pushed my right hand back against the Grizzly Bear fur; The **Shaman Kween** then abruptly turned to walk out towards the two tall Black Crushed Velvet Drapes on my left; I watched the splendor of the **Shaman Kween** slowly fade beyond the fabric as it hung from the ceiling's great height. Seconds after the **Shamans** exit, I no longer felt any pain in my shoulder as it felt completely healed, nor did I feel any further side effects from the fall I had from **The Cage of Glass** into the heated pool.

As of now, I only felt the room's tranquil atmosphere, and the side belly of heavy breathing from the sleeping Grizzly Bear I set against. Beyond all that, the live music remained soulfully smooth, and the crowd of raised hands continued to flicker with lights throughout the dimmed room. The cold snowflakes continued to fall as the heated pool gave its warmth; it was sort of like a warm bliss below but a pleasurable cold chill at the top… a type of vibe that was unpredictably comfortable. While lost in my thoughts, my eyes explored the room's fullness as I became distracted… and then without warning it happened! I felt the right index and middle finger of **Madam Mrs. Dame's** two right prints pressing securely against the center hairs of my chest. The warm edible oils and herbs dripped from her fingertips as she held the Brass Singing Bowl in her left hand.

I never even heard the **Madam** move towards me from the distance that she stood; I also noticed that there wasn't a drop of oil spilled from the Brass Singing Bowl when I looked down behind her at **The Glass Platform**. I couldn't figure out how she approached me so damn fast when I only looked away briefly. My focus was now **Madam Mrs. Dame's** black cherry lips erotically scatting to the live music beneath her breath. As her two fingers pressed harder against my Sternum. The oils from her fingers continued to drip down to my abdomen; warmly rolling down towards my bottom shaft to the ending hang of my under-crown's tip… on to **The Glass Platform**. I then asked the **Madam** the most obvious question; a question that any smart man should ask a woman of such eminence standing in front of one's predicament as such as this.

"So, what happens now…? *Madam!*"

Madam Mrs. Dame ceased her harmony of erotic scatting with a quick irritated laugh as she spoke with a grim tone.

"Oberon, the one with so many FUCKING QUESTIONS... HERE IS MY ONLY ANSWER TO THAT."

The *Madam* lifted her right hand from the center of my chest and savagely pressed the major pressure points in my face down to my feet, and rendered most of my mobility and speech. I was only able to feel, breathe, and move certain parts of my body as I laid back against the Grizzly Bear's sleeping body. The room of eyes acted as if none of this shit was happening while still enjoying this deceptive scheme of *Madam Mrs. Dame.* I felt like she was purposely trying to trigger me to get out of pocket. I felt pinned like a Voodoo Doll and stuck like sap to a tree but then three captivating Haitian women wearing Karabela Dresses with head wraps came from behind the two tall Black Crushed Velvet Drapes. The three women approached me to force my partially motionless body to kneel back down; two of the women held my arms outward and stretched. The other woman placed her right hand around my forehead and the left hand under my jaw.

Then out of nowhere the room of guest begins chanting a smooth meditation melody along with the live band's rhythm of naughty notes. I stared at *Madam Mrs. Dame* with fury as her feet got cleansed and soaked in the melted snowflakes as the vitality of her sexual magnetism pulled at my attention. As the three Haitian women held me tight and down on my knees, the woman behind me opened my mouth as she gripped my jaw tight and I grunted in agitation. The *Madam* then raised the Brass Singing Bowl high in the middle of us as she stood over me bowing my force. *Mrs. Dame* lifted her right leg placing some of her soft toes in my mouth, she lightly rested the bottom ball of her foot on my lower lip and bottom row of teeth. She grinned as she looked at me in my eyes taunting me with her lewd beauty.

My face was starting to shake with anger as I looked up at her from her toes in my mouth. Her skin was like *Black Forest Calla Lily's.* Her body and beauty would make any real man break his neck and ankles to see her alluring smile of furious nature. Furthermore, held in her left hand the shadow of the Brass Singing Bowl came over her raised right ankle. She gradually started to pour the prepped baste of edible oils and herbs upon her supple anklebone down the top arch of her foot. As I looked at her gorgeous toes drizzling the edible herbs and oils into the heat of my mouth; most of it ran down my body at the inner crease of my thigh. My mouth held most of what she poured. Then *Madam Mrs. Dame* gave me four words in a romantic tone.

"Surprise Your Madam, Oberon."

The room seemed like it was waiting for my resolution. Unable to move my full body after all the pressure points pressed to render most of my movement. So, I just did what was expected but with my twist to the erotic script that she was trying to convey into her head within this lewd reality. Beyond all that, I am more pissed that everyone I met tonight kept underestimating me but does not know the level of what I am capable of or who I am. So, I then let my tongue and lips do the basic work to detour *Madam Mrs. Dame* from forming more doubt in my actions.

As the spoken muscle of my mouth becomes an enigma upon her polished toes and flesh as I skip certain pressure points under her foot. Yet grazing her other points of pressure, I licked down gently with the whip of my taste buds; then I coursed towards her bottom heel pad, which is the 35th pressure point beneath her dripping foot of oils and herbs. The room watched my limited motion as I let my mouth, and neck handle her chocolate toes; down to her feet towards finally flipping the erotic coin on this divine woman. I tried to hit that damn 35th pressure point in her heel harshly with my tongue with ambitions that we all will grasp the *Madam's* sacred *Yoni's* aroma. I have already tasted the fresh Papaya from the high-ranking beautiful *Shaman Kween*, so I'm hoping to at least crack the seal on the ruling *Madam* of this place… even if it's just a single focused touch.

After the 35th pressure point was hit, *Madam Mrs. Dame* dropped the Brass Singing Bowl from her left hand; the bowl quickly hit *The Glass Platform* and rolled off into the vast heated pool. The *Madam* slowly removed her foot of dripping edible oils and herbs; she stepped back crossing her arms taken aback. She stood calm in her Leather Open Breast Full Body Harness Lingerie with her soft bottom line smiling. The whole damn room went instantly silent once again; they all stood up to walk closer to the heated pool surprised. I couldn't help but laugh loudly because then I smelled a new elegant fragrance of chocolate mint lingering from between her inner thighs. I knew then that the **Madam's Yoni** did not misinterpret my love language... at all! **Madam Mrs. Dame** did not foresee that chess move coming; as I watched her face become an art piece of a frowning sexiness with that slight sense of bravo and pleasure in her eyes.

Madam Mrs. Dame looked around the silent room at her garden of eyes gazing at us nearby, and the three captivating Haitian women held me tighter. My knees felt numb against **The Glass Platform** but I didn't give two flights of a fuck as long as I proved my point. Even without having full control of my body I still didn't fall apart under all that came at me so why falter now? I now consider this all, many pleasures of lessons beyond all sensual brutality. **Madam Mrs. Dame** then looked down at me, and then up at one of the three Haitian women and winked with her right eye.

Then the enticing Haitian woman on my left took her right hand and reset all my pressure points giving my body its full movement. Then the other two Haitian women released their hold of me; my body fell forward well I caught myself with both hands pressing to **The Glass Platform** beneath my naked body. The **Madam** sucked her teeth loudly and the three Haitian women began to walk away in a straight line from which they came. As I watched the three lovely women walk away; I then wiped the remaining edible oils and herbs from the hair of my face with my left forearm and swallowed the rest. The taste of it was like the syrup sweetness of Gaia going down the wetness of my throat. Before I could stand to my feet, **Madam Mrs. Dame** squatted down in front of me; with her left hand firmly rubbing down the right top of my face down to the side hairs of my beard. This woman smelled appetizingly unavoidable, especially with her **Yoni** positioned much closer to me with that sweet procrastinating fragrance of chocolate mint. Her knees were bent outward and down to her sides; her bouncing bust was centered in my sight with her words speaking at me.

"Oberon, know this, you may have agitated a veiled part of my body by revealing the potency of my Yoni's door while surprising me with your hidden skill. You may have ambushed me, and stolen a whiff of

my unforgettable aroma of chocolate mint but that is all your spontaneous ass will receive from this Kween, for I am the Madam overall. At some point, you will be punished by my hands for ruining my lingerie without my consent to turn on the waters of my falls. Until I decide that punishment, Oberon, I... Madam Mrs. Dame... welcome you to my home, completely. Mrs. Sweet Dame's Nightspot is my imperium but we are more than what you see; you just happen to drop by on the one night we had off of certain duties. This was a very important day off from handling the real business of heavy artillery and much more which you have no choice but to know of.

You could never over-prove your loyalty to us... Always keep reaching high here. You will never have to worry about any of us clipping your wings, yet we will be soaring with you taking you to heights of greater circumstances. I am now your Divine Madam, as I am there's, and we always protect our own and many others but tonight, know that you are safe. Also, you didn't think I would reward you by letting you have some of my succulent chamber of wishes, did you? Mmmm, you couldn't have thought that now, Oberon. What I have is not to be earned but untouched until I demand it to be felt by whom I deem qualified at that time. Enough talk, Oberon, just have fun celebrating tonight."

Madam Mrs. Dame leaned in and kissed me on the mere lining of my top lip, it was feather light but so warm to the touch. The *Madam* removed her hand from the side of my face and stood up as she sauntered away towards the two tall Black Crushed Velvet Drapes. I most definitely watched her walk away while she was jiggling with strength in her steps. As I sat with my knees on the floor of the glass unable to look away from the *Madam Mrs. Dame's* body at my left distance. Her exquisiteness vanished behind the drapes, and that same beautifully loud bird whistle was heard beyond the soft Black Crushed Velvet; after the whistling sounded off, *Prudence* woke up without hesitation while shaking the snowflakes from its thick coat. Without any distraction, the Grizzly Bear calmly walked away towards the *Madam's* beautiful call. As *Prudence* leaves *The Glass Platform* vanishing into the drapes the silent room cheers loudly; everyone looks pleased with how smooth everything went.

I felt completely burned out as I finally stood to my feet but fatigued or not, I believe I stepped outside of my box a great deal. As I looked around the room the snowflakes no longer fell, and the lights in the room brightened just a bit; the live band jazzed up the music with a laid-back upbeat type of feel. I felt free in my naked body as I looked at the lights above me. Then I looked up and I watched a brown silk robe drop from the ceiling shadows. I reached out to grasp it with my left hand, and noticed **Prudence's** embroidered paw print was on the front left side of it; my name was under it with numbers *777* next to it. I did know that *777* meant to release all fears and represent inner strength. So, I placed it upon my body and slowly walked towards the wooden ramp because I damn sure needed a strong drink after this and something to eat.

I stepped off **The Glass Platform** onto the wooden ramp as the cheers continued to roar but started to settle as I neared the end of the ramp. **Slender'Guava** met me at its end with her right hand on her hip and kept her left behind her back. I stepped onto the main floor in front of **Slender'Guava** with the **"What Now"** look written on my face and from behind her back she had handed me a glass of Bourbon as she spoke.

"Oberon, don't look like that, you know you want this drink after all of that beloved, plus you look like you started enjoying the process but I guess I could be wrong."

I looked at **Slender'Guava** and just laughed because she was telling me nothing but the truth. I nodded my head in agreeance with a slick grin on my face but I was kind of mad I didn't get a session in with the Grand **Madam**, maybe one day. I looked to **Slender'Guava** with a question.

"Slender'Guava, I know this might be weird to ask but what happens now… like, for real this time."

She looked at me laughing…**"Oberon, whatever you want as long as you don't break the rules and keep things sexy and grown because tonight is all about feeling good. You look like you are about done for tonight anyway my love. Why don't you just get some rest in one of the rooms in the sleeping quarters below this floor, this place is bigger than you would ever believe. I will have someone walk you to your room to get cleaned up so you can rest, and you can just leave** *when you get up love but remember you can stay as long as you like now. Also, if you are hungry, you can order it from your room, I will have them take you down to the next level... it's never a problem to do extra because we take care of each other here."*

I looked into the pretty eyes of **Slender'Guava** and replied **"Forgive me but Hell Yeah, that's what I'm talking about, let's do that sweet love!"** *Slender'Guava* signaled over a pretty Filipino woman in a purple bikini to walk me to my room; this nice woman was kind enough to just take my order as we walked to the room, which was nothing but a tasty **Bourbon Glazed Salmon Cesar Salad**. While my food was being prepared, I took a hot shower and cleaned up. I sat at the end of the bed in my drying towel waiting until I received a knock at the door, and I replied.

"Come In."

The waitress came in with a sexy smile and placed my food on the table across the way next to this nice long mirror built into the wall. I walked over to the table and sat down and started eating while I collected my thoughts. My mind was overwhelmed and excited at the same damn time. After eating my food I felt tapped out, I was surprised I didn't pass out while eating at the table. As I stood up to walk to my bed, and then the room lights went out and the large mirror behind me began to shine with green and gold lights. I looked back and the **superior receptionist Iguana** stood there wearing a **forest green Sheer Black Kaftan;** she calmly laughed with her sexy dimples and braces set across her lovely smile. Her pompadour was undone, and down to her shoulders as she spoke to me from the double shining mirror of lights.

"I hope that your first day was not too harsh on you because it's not like that all the time... only when newcomers arrive here. Most people we don't know usually don't make it past the front door of the building but I guess Madam Mrs. Dame took a risk with you for some reason. Anyhow, I do inner stand that you are tired but you wouldn't leave a woman like me unbothered, without at least giving a lady the attention that she deserves. You are a romantic gentleman, aren't you, Oberon?"

"Yes, Iguana, I know I'm a gentleman but I am burnt out *Kween*."

"Oberon, I do not need sex my dear but I do want you to hold me until we fall to sleep."

"*Iguana,* I can do that, just come out from the mirror and let us reflect our hold, and rest."

"**Oberon,** that sounds marvelous but just know you owe me in the grand rising."

"No problem, *Iguana*, what's the best that can happen!"

"Ooooh... yes!"

WELCOME TO,

The Serenaders Lounge...

THE ARTIST SPOT LIGHT PRESENTS

Author Poet Katrina McCain

"Write In Peace"

Author/ Poet
Katrina A. McCain
October 28, 1976 ~ June 9, 2024

Published Books:
"One Day Things Changed: One Day Things Changed: Fictional Short Stories of Love, Betrayal, and Redemption **"- 2023**
"Then The Unexpected Happened"- 2021
"Because She Decided to Love: Poems on Love & Relationship *" – 2020*

Website:
www.poetkatrinamccain.com

Before turning the page to lay eyes upon such a sensational poetic piece written by *Author Poet Katrina A. McCain*, I must give this poetic legend her flowers of ultimate respect. *Katrina* is a deep-hearted sister that I and my wife love and appreciate as family and friends of four-plus years. I crossed my sister's path on social media upon being impressed by her poetry writing skills. A while back I sent my sister a follow-on IG, followed by a positive direct message and we have been family since 2019. I also thank her for trusting me to create the book cover and interior design for two out of three of her published masterpieces, *"Because She Decided to Love" and "One Day Things Changed"* which I enjoyed designing.

Author/Poet Katrina A. McCain has three incredible books published before she left this world to be at peace. Thank you for just being the awesome person that you are, and I appreciate you for writing a poetic piece so that I may feature your skills to be shown to others who will respect your art as I do. I would like my powerful sister to end my book with her awesome words. We miss and love you to life for always being a supportive and loving sister that I and my Ultimate Kween Wife are happy to call family. I will keep your legacy alive my sister, always. *Katrina,* I wish that you could have seen my second Masterpiece before ever transitioning, you were super motivational all the time. Thank you for the poetic donation you sent me, and thank you for trusting, and believing in me. Let's turn the page and admire the poetic style of one of my favorite Authors.

"Time Stood Still"
Author Poet Katrina A. McCain

Arguing, fussing, and fighting for months now;
I didn't want to face you after work this evening.

No more errands left to run or stalling left to do,
I headed home expecting round 10 of verbal combat.

Puzzled at how we got where we don't communicate,
I would rather go to bed than figure it out though.

Hearing our favorite song playing as I exited the car,
I thought about our First Dance 8 years ago.

Time stood still as I was thinking about our wedding night activities.

Seeing the dim lights, flowers, chocolate, and you;
I smiled when I walked through the front door.

Pain etched across your face as you grabbed me,
I let you guide me to you while unsure of what was happening.

Holding me tightly and telling me we could fix things,
I felt safe in your arms for the first time in a while.

Fighting back tears that showed up weekly now,
I was ecstatic that they joined us under different circumstances.
Time stood still at the thought of us being back to us again.
Asking me to put everything aside and recommit to you,
I agreed and trusted this safe space you were creating.

Candles lined every inch of the staircase and our bedroom,
I saw a bath which was drawn for me already and I needed this.

Turning around to thank you for being so considerate,
I didn't realize you were behind me with a glass of wine.

Submerging myself in the best water I have ever felt,
I wanted you to join me, but I couldn't take any rejection.

Time stood still between us, but baby come to me and make it all
good.

Breathing deeply to rid the night of negativity and prejudgment,
I opened my eyes when I felt tender kisses on my neck.

My head was swimming from the intoxication of you,
I only had one glass of wine that couldn't take the credit.

Admiring how gracefully you are aging and how sexy you are,
I am fortunate that you are mine despite the difficult times.

Lifting me to rest on your unrobed body in the water,
I felt sensational, sexy, hot, desired, erotic, and amazing.

Time stood still with each splash of water hitting the floor.

Our pace quickened as you wrapped your arms around my thighs,
I lost my mind as you drove deeper with determination.

Demanding me to open my eyes so I could see you as I felt you,
I struggled to focus on your command which I used to love to do.

Your stimulating voice controlled how nasty our lovemaking
intensified.

Pleasantly landing on your chest after a couple of releases,
I saved one last hoorah for you just the way I know you like it.
Time stood still as we aggressively sealed the deal on what was
needed.

WELCOME TO,
The Serenaders Lounge...
THE LIMNER SPOT LIGHT PRESENTS

Bertrina Shorter
ImaginationArts78

Website:
www.imaginationarts78.com

Social Media:
(Instagram, Facebook, TikTok, YouTube)
@imaginationarts78

There are so many unique painters in this world who are masters of their craft, and I happened to come across one; I searched very hard for someone with art that speaks the visual energy of my classy erotica book. **Bertrina Shorter** is a master of her craft, and a living legend with an exquisite style of fine art that speaks natural volumes of power, depth, and limitless imagination which is shown in her illustrations.

I appreciate **Bertrina Shorter** for taking the time to allow me to showcase this beautiful painting that she has created from within her mind of great ideas. Beyond being a marvelous painter, she is also a very down-to-earth, and respectful person that all will soon get to know more through her work and achievements. I thank you royal one for such a wonderful canvas of art that you gifted to us all.

Bertrina Shorter

"ImaginationArts78"

Painting Titled:
Twisted Silhouette

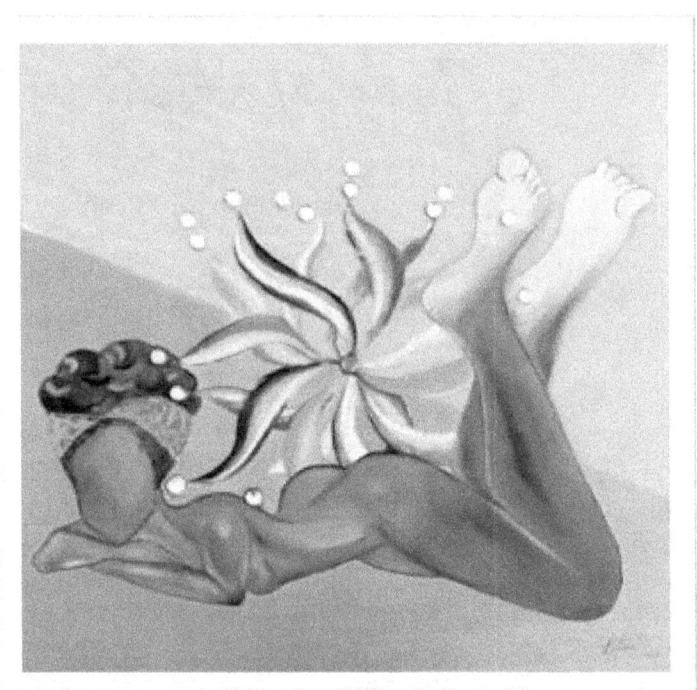

Author

The Poet B.GKL

I was born on December 28, 1986, and raised in Detroit, MI. I have always been most known for being a multi-talented triple threat when it comes to entertainment. Being able to switch from Hip Hop, Neo-Soul & R&B, and never forgetting to be the pure poetic writer that I have grown to become. I am a black hole of hidden artistry, and I take glory in all the crafts I hold with a humble hand of strength.

My main goal is to build, network, and collaborate with unique talents from all races of people, and bring different minds together to create incredible short stories and art; my biggest skill is bringing anything I write or due to life while breaking the boundaries of all writing limits.

Sincerely, *The Poet B.GKL* aka *Brotha GKL / Gawd Keenng Lio'lf*

Professional:
Writer, Author, Poet, Narrator, Graphic Designer, Photographer, Videographer & Audio Editor, Script Writer, Actor, Artist Developer, Motivational Speaker, Ghost Writer, Social Media Marketer, Neo-Soul Singer, Hip Hop Artist, Studio Recording Engineer, and Model.

Website:
www.authorbgkl.com
www.cvaughnk.com

Sites:
https://linktr.ee/Thepoet_BrothaGKL
https://linktr.ee/MrAndMrsKaigler
https://linktr.ee/CvaughnKphotography

Email:
Thepoet-b.gkl@hotmail.com

Business:
C'vaughn'K Graphic Designs
(313) 334-9630

CirAngleSquare
"Levels of Trust"
Art Design By: Gawd Keenng Lio'lf

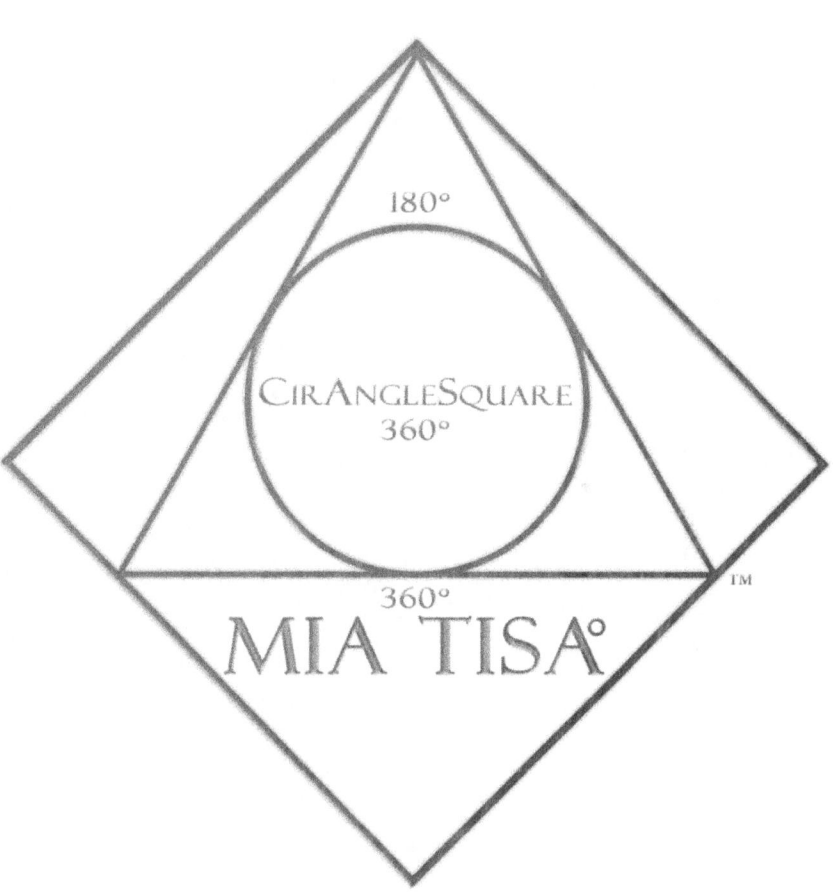